PREACHER

FURY VIPERS MC: DUBLIN
BOOK 1

BROOKE SUMMERS

First Edition published in 2024

Text Copyright © Brooke Summers

Edits by Farrant Editing

Proofreading by Author bunnies

All rights reserved.

The moral right of the author has been asserted. No part of this publication may be reproduced, stored in or introduced into a retrieval system, or transmitted, in any form or by any means (electronic, mechanical, photocopying, recording or otherwise), nor be otherwise circulated in any form of binding or cover other than that in which it is published without the prior written permission of the author. Any person who does any unauthorized act in relation to this publication may be liable to criminal prosecution and civil claims for damages.

All characters in this publication are fictitious and any resemblance to real persons, living or dead, is purely coincidental.

CONTENT
PLEASE READ CAREFULLY.

There are elements and themes within this book that some readers might find extremely upsetting.

Please click here (https://brookesummersbooks.com/contentwarnings/) for that list of potentially harmful topics. Please heed these as this book contains some heavy topics that some readers could find damaging.

PROLOGUE
PREACHER

"Bro, are you sure you're going to be okay?" Garret asks as we walk quickly toward the house.

I grit my teeth and nod. There's no way I'd say otherwise. "Yeah, I'll be fine," I lie.

He gives me a look that tells me he doesn't believe me. Garret has been my best friend since we were seven. He knows how fucked up my family is. He knows that when I go home tonight, it's not going to be pretty. In fact, I have no doubt that tonight is going to be one of the worst nights of my life.

Lately, my father has been getting worse. He hates when anyone talks back to him and he despises it when I'm late. Which I am. I'm seventeen minutes late at the moment and we're almost home. I couldn't help it. My truck's battery died about two miles away from home, and I knew if I didn't leave it where it was, I'd be even later than I am now.

"I'll have Dad tow your truck once I'm home," Garret says as he runs a hand through his shaggy hair. "Kane, your father's going to hit the roof. We both know what he's like when you miss your curfew."

Oh boy, do we both know what he gets like. Broken bones, busted lips, and bloody noses are among his favorite injuries to cause when he really gets going.

"I'll be fine. I appreciate your father getting my truck, man. Tell him I'll pay him whatever it is I owe when I'm ungrounded." I sigh.

"Two weeks, bro. You've got two weeks and then we can get the hell out of this fucked up town."

I nod. I'm counting down the days. I can't fucking wait. It's been a long time coming. The sooner I get out of this hick of a fucked up town, the better. "Do your parents know that we're going?"

Garret grins. "Yep. They're coming with us," he says. "They've wanted to be gone for years, but they've been waiting until we hit eighteen. You know that everyone in town knows what goes on in your house, right?"

"Yeah," I say, slightly defeated. It's fucked up that every grown-ass adult knows that the pastor beats the fuck out of his kids and not one of them do anything to stop him.

We reach my house, and the porch light is on. I take a steadying breath and turn to Garret.

"See you in two weeks," I tell him with a slight chuckle. I'm going to be grounded for the rest of the summer, but the moment I turn eighteen, I'm gone, and there's no stopping me. Not anymore.

He gives me a grin. "See you in two weeks, Kane."

I shove my hands into my pockets and move toward the steps. Before I reach the top step, the front door opens, revealing my father standing in the doorway. His green eyes are dark and filled with anger, his lips twisted, and his weathered face contorted with so much rage, I know the beating I'm about to get is going to be one of the worst I've ever had.

He reaches for me, his thick fingers curling around my shoulder, and drags me toward him.

"The fuck are you playing at?" he spits as he pushes me into the house, slamming the front door closed behind us. "You just have to push your luck all the damn time, don't you? Hmm? I told you your curfew was six-thirty, and what time is it now? Almost seven." He pulls his arm back and brings it forward, snapping his meaty fist into my face. "You are such a disappointment," he shouts.

He lands blow after blow to my face and abdomen. He's a heavy man. He's not lean or overly muscular, but he's got a lot of weight behind his punches. Over the past two years, I've bulked up a lot. I've gained fifty pounds of muscle, so I'm able to cope with his blows a lot more. But sometimes he manages to land a hit that drops me to my knees. He's a tall fucker who loves to bully people he deems to be beneath him.

"Where were you?" Mom asks, her eyes wide as she watches her fucked up husband beat me. Yet again.

"My truck broke down. I had to walk two miles," I say, coughing through the pain. "Garret was with me. He's going to get his dad to tow my truck for me."

Mom's expression shifts from wide-eyed and sad, to angry, her eyes narrowing.

"Seriously?" she says with a shake of her head. "Why do you always lie, Kane? Why can't you just tell the truth for once in your life?"

She's just as bad as Dad. She always eggs him on, making stupid comments to get me into trouble. She's the perfect pastor's wife, all about faith and appearances. Yet everyone knows how fucked up both of them are.

"You know what the Lord said about lying, son," Dad says thickly, his voice filled with rage. "The LORD detests lying lips, but he delights in people who are trustworthy," he snarls. "Proverbs chapter twelve: verse twenty-two."

He throws yet another punch, and I'm unable to block it or dodge it. This one connects with my nose, which cracks beneath the force. The impact reverberates around my skull, creating a hideous sound.

Blood spurts from my nose and fills my mouth, the metallic taste has always been something that I hate. I spit the blood from my lips and glare at my father. I hate this man.

"Fathers, do not provoke your children to anger, but bring them up in the discipline and instruction of the Lord," I say in return. "Ephesians chapter six verse four."

"Are you talking back to me?" he snarls. "You dare to challenge my words?"

I stare at him, every ounce of hate that I have for him pours out of me like an open wound. There's no one I hate more than the man that raised me. "I'm not challenging your words. I'm merely conveying what the Lord has said," I say, knowing that it's going to rile him up even more. "You're all about serving the Lord, our Savior, but you do not do as he says. Instead, you abuse your children, and have your wife follow by example. There will be no Heaven for you, Father, only Hell, and I pray to God that you burn when you get there."

I knew it was coming, but bracing wasn't enough to prepare me for the onslaught that ensues. Punch after punch after punch, he doesn't stop. The hits are hard and punishing. It doesn't take me long to realize that it's not just my father who's attacking me, but my mother also.

"You need to repent," my father spits. "Repent for your sins, give your life to the Lord and he shall repay you. Go against the Lord and you shall suffer the consequences."

"You need to learn, Kane. Seek solace in the Lord and let him guide you. Let him show you the path to forgiveness and righteousness. If you don't, you'll end up in Hell," Mom says harshly.

"Fuck you," I hiss, blood pooling in my mouth. "If Heaven has you two in it, I'd rather go to Hell. Then again, do you honestly believe that either of you are going to fucking Heaven?" I chuckle. "No, you two are going to the depths of Hell, right next to child predators and murderers."

"You liar," Mom screams. "You dirty rotten liar."

I hear the sound of my father's belt buckle, and I know the beatings are about to get a whole lot worse. Fuck these bastards and their bullshit. Two more weeks and then I'm out of here, and I'll never have to see either of these fuckers again.

"You need to wash your mouth out, son," my father snaps as he whips the belt across my back.

I learned a long time ago not to cry out in pain. That only fuels the fire within my parents and makes them extend the beating. Instead, I bow my head and take the pain, twisting it to rage. I know that one day, I'll lose control of the rage bottled up inside of me, and I'll end up hurting someone. I pray that someone is my father.

Movement in my peripheral vision catches my attention, and I turn slightly to see my brother standing in the doorway, tears streaming down his face as he watches our parents beat me. He's only fourteen years old. I've tried to shield him as much as I possibly can from their brutality, but sometimes it's not enough. They get to him when I'm not around. It seems they've been on one today, as Abel's got a busted lip and his nose is bloodied. He hates them just as much as I do. Leaving him behind is going to be hard, but I have to. There's no other choice. I have to leave him behind for my own sanity. I can't stay here. If I do, I'm going to end up dead or killing someone, and neither is an option for me. Not yet anyway.

"Stop it!" Abel screams at them. "Stop hurting him. He's right, you're evil. You're both pure evil. Our Lord wouldn't want you at his side in Heaven. He'd look down on you in Hell with disgust."

"Boy," my father snarls. "Stay the fuck out of this. It's between your brother and us."

"No," Abel says. "It's not. You're the worst parents in the world and I hate you. Everyone in this town knows how fucked up you both are. Everyone hates you. But because you're the pastor, there's nothing they can do about it. You ever wonder why the conversations stop whenever you walk into a room?" he taunts them. "That's because you're the conversation. It's about you and how fucked up you are for hurting your boys. They all think you're hypocrites. Preaching about love and forgiveness but beating your boys until they can't move. You're the talk of the town."

"You dare," our mother screeches at him. "You dare lie."

I chuckle, unable to hold back. "He's not lying. Come on, Mother, you know he's not lying."

The belt hisses through the air as my father brings it down across my back. I bite back a pained groan. He's cut through the skin. I can feel the blood pooling in the wound. Fuck.

"Carry on, Abel, and your brother is going to feel a lot more pain," he goads.

Fuck, this is new. Usually, they'll beat one of us and move on to the next. It seems as though they've found a new way to torture us both. They know we don't want the other hurting. Sick fucking bastards.

"Fine," Abel snaps. "Just so you know, my nightly prayers consist of me praying for your death. Every fucking night." He turns on his heel and moves to his room, slamming the door as he does. I smile when I hear the snick of his lock engaging.

"Get up," Father shouts. "Get the fuck up and get out of my sight. I'm not finished with you yet."

I roll my eyes. Of course he isn't.

"Don't think this is the end. You carry on with that backtalk, boy, and that bike that's in that garage will end up in a landfill," Dad snarls.

Damn the asshole. He's really starting to find new and creative ways to make both Abel and I compliant. I have a Harley Davision Cruiser. It's taken me two years to restore it to its former glory. She's one of the best bikes money can buy. I saved up to get it, both my parents hated it, but there was nothing they could do about it. I'm not allowed to ride until I'm eighteen, but it's fully restored and waiting for me to come of age.

It takes me a lot longer than I would have hoped to get to my feet and move away from him, but I manage to make it to my room. The second my door is closed, I flip the lock. Our parents don't have keys to them. Oh, they'll be pissed that they can't come in, but it'll give both Abel and I time to heal from the beatings.

I collapse onto my bed and release a muffled groan into my pillow. Fuck. I'm in so much fucking pain. I won't be able to move again for a while.

It doesn't take long until I pass out from the pain.

CHAPTER 1
PREACHER

EIGHTEEN MONTHS LATER

"The fuck?" I growl as I see some asshole looking at my bike.

The asshole in question raises his head and turns to me. He's got a fucking smirk on his face. "Didn't touch it, man. Just admirin' its beauty."

"Best keep it that way," I snap.

The asshole raises his hands as I step closer to him, I notice a scar on his eyebrow, one that reminds me of Abel and my heart clenches at the thought of my brother. Christ, it's been eighteen months and my past is still raw. There's not a day that goes by that I don't think about what happened to both Abel and I.

It's been eighteen months since I left that God forsaken house, and I haven't looked back. I'll die before I ever step foot back there again. Ain't no fucking way I'd ever willingly go back. My parents can rot for all I care.

Since I left, my life has gone to shit. I escaped with Garret and his parents. It was easy to do as we left during one of my father's services. What with the beatings that I took in the two weeks leading up to my birthday I wasn't allowed to be seen. My parents lost their ever-loving shit during that time period and didn't give a fuck about keeping up pretences any longer. They repeatedly whaled on me and beat me until I was unconscious. It was fucking brutal. When Garret and his parents arrived, I could barely hold myself up. Thankfully, they helped me into my truck and Garret drove it for me as we got the fuck out of town.

It was hard leaving that house. The morning of my departure, Abel committed suicide. He couldn't stay in that house any longer. He took his life because he was stuck with our parents. He knew I was leaving because I told him. I wouldn't have left without warning him. But I was leaving him behind, even after he begged me to take him with me. The guilt from that decision has plagued me for the past eighteen months, and will continue to until the day I die. Had I not left, Abel would still be alive.

Our parents acted as though nothing had happened. They went about their day without a second thought. Bastards.

Garret and his family cared for me until I was able to stand on my own two feet. But with the pain I was feeling and the guilt that was burning inside of me, I couldn't stay around them. I thanked them and left Boston. I owe them my life, but they're a reminder of everything that's happened. I moved to New York and haven't spoken to them since.

Since then, I've lost my way somewhat. I don't go to college, nor do I feel the need to. I don't have a purpose in life, and I'm struggling to find my feet. I've turned into an asshole and I can't help it. The anger I feel is something I can't get rid of. It's so deeply ingrained in me that it flows through me as easily as my blood does.

"Want to calm the fuck down, man? I was lookin'. I didn't touch. Damn... Who the fuck pissed in your Wheaties this mornin'?"

I glare at the bastard, but he's not fazed one bit. "Is there a reason you're annoying the ever-loving shit out of me?"

His grin widens. "Nope. It's not my fault you woke

up on the wrong side of the bed. Besides, I was just admirin' your bike. That's all. You can do the same with mine if you'd like. She's a whole lot better than yours."

That's utter bullshit. No one has a better bike than mine. She's one of the best bikes money can buy. I worked every chance I had on it as I was growing up. I spare a glance at his and realize he's got the exact same fucking bike as me.

"Did you restore it?" I ask him, and he nods. "Cool. Same."

"You're not from around here, are you?" he asks. "Your accent is a huge giveaway. You're from the south, right?"

I nod. "Yep. You're not from here either. Where are you from?"

"Raleigh. My name's Todd."

"Kane," I reply, still skeptical about this guy.

"What brings you to New York?"

I lift my shoulders. "Needed a change. You?"

"Searchin' for somethin'. Don't know what, but I'm hopin' I'll find it. You ever heard of the Vipers?"

I blink. "Vipers?"

"Brother," he says with a shake of his head. "You're in New York and you've never heard of the Fury Vipers MC?"

I shake my head. No, I've never heard of them. "Who are they?"

He crosses his arms over his chest. "I met a guy a couple of weeks ago. His road name is Ace. He's a member of the motorcycle club. He gave me the whole spiel, but honestly, brother, the thing that sold it to me was the belongin'. I ain't belonged to somethin' in a fuckin' long time, and Ace said there's a whole brotherhood in that club. He invited me to come along and meet them, get a feel for them and them me. If the brothers like me, then I can become a prospect for the club. I'm goin' tonight. I can bring a friend. You want to come?"

"Why the fuck does this sound cultish?" I ask, wondering where the hell this fucker's going to lead me. The way he's making it sound, it's as though they're going to get me to the club and make me sign my rights away in blood.

He chuckles. "Nah, it's not a cult. They own the auto shop in the Bronx."

My eyes widen when I realize who he means. "Fury's Auto Shop?"

He nods. "That's the one."

"So, what—we go to the club, have a few drinks, and meet a few of the brothers? Then what?"

"The brothers will decide if you're the right guy to prospect with them."

I shake my head. "I dunno, man, it still sounds kind of sus to me."

Ain't no way I'm getting tied up with anything remotely close to a cult, especially after the shit I put up with from my parents. No fucking way.

"Check it out and then see. As far as I can tell, you'd get along with them."

I grit my teeth, feeling uneasy, I don't know anything about these guys, but I'm intrigued. I want to know what they're about. "Maybe."

He chuckles. "Meet me at the clubhouse tonight and check it out." He turns on his heel and moves to his bike. I watch him go, wondering who the fuck he is and what the hell the Fury Vipers are.

"Yo, Kane, you made it," Todd says as he staggers over to me.

I instantly regret coming here, especially with this ass. He's so drunk, he can't even walk in a straight line. He's messy as fuck and it's not a good look.

"What the fuck, man?" I hiss as he reaches me. "The fuck are you drunk for?"

"I'm chillin' with the guys."

"Man," I hear from beside me. I turn and see a tall

guy with tattoos covering his neck and hands glaring at Todd. "You want to get rid of him. He's a fuck up."

I raise a brow at him. "And you are?"

He grins. "My name's Grayson, but everyone calls me Reaper."

"Oh, and why's that?" I ask.

"'Cause when I'm around, death's coming."

"Are you a member?" I ask. I get the sense he's a guy I would like, he's no nonsense and shoots straight. Todd has pissed me the fuck off already, by being a drunken fuck, he's so loud, and I don't want to be dealing with his drunken ass tonight. I barely know the guy and he's already started some bullshit for me.

He shakes his head. "Not yet. I'm a prospect, and let me tell you, it's the best decision I made. But if you want to be a prospect too, you gotta lose the guy. He's a fuck up. There's no way the brothers are going to allow him to stay. He needs to leave."

"I just met this guy today. I don't know who the fuck he is. He told me to come along tonight, but fuck, he's not a friend." If the prospect can see he's a mess, what the fuck are the other guys thinking?

Reaper nods. "Alright, man, I hear you. Want a drink?"

"Sounds good," I reply.

Reaper introduces me to the brothers, letting them all know that while Todd invited me, I don't know him.

The brothers get rid of Todd, and all of them tell me how much of an ass the fucker is. They were glad to get rid of him. The only reason he was allowed to stay was because he was talking about his friend coming and how great I was. When they found out that I didn't know the ass, they banished him from the club.

The night wears on and I kick back and chat with the guys. They talk about bikes and the auto shop the club owns, and then, of course, the women come out, and fuck, there are enough to go around. But I stay back. I'm not in the mood to do that. I don't know these guys and I want to keep my wits about me.

"You headed home now, brother?" Reaper asks.

I nod. "Yeah."

"Be back tomorrow," Ace tells me as he walks toward the back of the clubhouse. "You're our newest prospect."

Reaper grins at me. "Fuck yeah. Told you, man."

"What time tomorrow?" I ask, wondering what the fuck I've got myself in for.

"Early," Ace shouts with a chuckle. "You're both cleanin' this shit up."

I glance around the clubhouse and see the mess that litters the floor and tables. Christ...

"Tomorrow," I say with a little sigh.

Reaper grins. "Don't worry, man, it'll be fine. Get

through the prospect era and then you're a patched member."

"How long does that take?" I ask.

He lifts his shoulders and shrugs. "Varies from guy to guy. But the average is around eight months."

That's doable. "I'll see you tomorrow then, man."

He grins as he flicks his two fingers out in a half-ass wave.

EIGHT YEARS LATER

My life has changed drastically over the past eight years. I'm no longer the kid who had no purpose. I found it the night I walked into the clubhouse of the Fury Vipers, and it wasn't long until I became a whole new man. I left Kane in the past where he belonged, and I became Preacher. My dislike for religion gave me my moniker, but I don't care. It's fitting, a fuck you to those two bastards who brought me into this world.

I glance down at the boy in my arms, and my heart swells but also breaks. Tyson was the best thing that ever happened to me. I had a son, one that I love with every fucking beat of my heart. His birth was beyond fucked up. His mom was a cunt. She was the lowest of the low when it comes to women. Drinking, doing drugs, and fucking multiple men bareback while the kid was growing in her uterus. I have no doubt that she would have killed the kid had she had the choice. From the second I found out my child was growing inside of her, I kept her on lockdown. She wanted to become an old lady, to become something she could never be. Not because she was a club whore, but because she was a raving fucking bitch. I'd have had no problems making her my old lady had she not been so fucking disgusting.

My son was born an addict. I think that was the most heartbreaking moment of my life. Never did I expect to see a new born baby fighting an addiction his mother had given him. It was brutal and it was fucked up. But I didn't leave his side. I made sure that he was okay, and that he wasn't alone. He's a fucking fighter—hence his name. He showed the world that he was born to fight, and he came out on top. Now, he's thriving.

Of course, my life can't go easy. No, there's always something that'll come along and fuck it up, and this time it was thanks to Mayhem. My brother meant well and I hold no grudges against him, but fuck, he pulled the rug from under me with the revelation that he blurted out.

Tyson's not my son.

Crack. My fucking world fell apart at his words. Not only is Tyson not my son, but he's Reaper's. My brother is the fucking best man I know, and the fact that he was willing to step back and let me continue to raise Tyson as my own says a fucking lot about who he is. But Reaper has done more than enough for me. The man went to prison for me. He served four years for me. I can't take Tyson from him. Not now that I know. Had it been anyone else, I would have left with the kid and never looked back. But right now, I have to do what's best for Tyson and Reaper, and that's letting them be together.

I hold Tyson tight in my arms, knowing this is the last time. There's no coming back after this. Heaviness settles on my chest as I look down at his chubby cheeks and big eyes.

How do I give him up and walk away?

I have no choice. I really don't. Reaper has already given up so much for me. I can't take his son from him.

"Little man," I say softly, my throat closing with emotion. "I'm so fuckin' sorry, but I have to go. I have no other choice. But you're goin' to be fine. You're gonna have the best parents to take care of you. Your dad is the best man I know, and your mom... well, your mom is the sweetest woman and she makes the best baked goods. They're going to love you and care for you."

I press a kiss to his head and hold him close to me. I inhale his scent, taking it in, knowing that it's the last fucking time. Christ... This is without a doubt the hardest thing I'm ever going to do.

There's a knock on the door and I open it to see Ace's old lady, Eda, standing in the doorway with a small smile on her face.

"Hey, you wanted to see me?" she asks, her voice raspy. She almost died when she was seven, and in doing so her voice box was damaged, which led to her raspy voice.

"Can you watch Tyson for a while?"

She doesn't hesitate to answer. "Of course." She reaches for him, and it takes every ounce of strength that I have to hand my boy over to her. "You know the kids love Tyson, as do I. I'm happy to watch him whenever you like."

"Thanks," I say, my voice rough.

She beams at me, and I watch as she takes my boy out of my room, closing the door behind her as she does. I can't help the tears that fall from my eyes. He's gone, and I'm never going to see him again.

Tonight, I leave. It's the best thing for everyone. There's no way I'd be able to live around them and watch as other people raised him and I know if I stay, Reaper is going to find it hard to do what needs to be done.

I've booked a flight. It leaves in a few hours. I'm leaving the US and I'm flying to Ireland. I'm not leaving the Vipers. I can't lose everything, so I'm doing the next best thing. I'm going to our Dublin chapter to escape.

I just pray it fucking works.

CHAPTER 2
PREACHER

TWO WEEKS LATER

"Preacher." I hear the Irish drawl of Denis Gallagher and turn to see the grayish-haired man walking toward me. He's in his mid-forties and has a fucking slew of children. One of which is my brother, Pyro's, old lady. Chloe is the fucking shit. Every brother adores her. She's perfect for Pyro and she makes him happy. Her parents have been integral in getting the clubhouse here in Dublin set up so that our chapter could have somewhere to live.

"Denis," I reply.

"It's good to see you, man. Shame about the circumstances, but I'm glad to have you here with us."

My blood turns ice-cold. Fuck, being away from Tyson is the hardest thing I've ever done. Especially with Wrath's old lady giving birth the moment I landed in Dublin. Being around a newborn brings back a fuck ton of memories that I've been trying to escape.

"What's up?" I ask, my tone not unfriendly, but there's definitely an edge to it.

"Three of my kids aren't biologically mine," he tells me, and it's something that I did, in fact, know. His ex-wife was a raging bitch. She gave Tyson's mom, Pepper, a run for the title of biggest cunt. I'm actually not entirely sure who'd win that, but thankfully, both women are dead and can no longer fuck up their kids' lives.

"Sorry to hear that, man, but you've got to realize that our situations aren't the same." He got to keep the kids that aren't his. He's raised them into adults and will continue to raise them. He's their father. I'm not Tyson's. My son will never know me as his father. It's the right thing to do, but it fucking kills me to be without him. I'm fucking dying inside and there's no way out of this deep, dark hole I'm falling into.

"That's true," he says with a nod. "But you've got to realize that you could still be involved in his life. You may not be called father, but you will always be his uncle, and while that's different, maybe when the scars heal, you'll feel the connection to him."

"You think it'll be that easy?"

"No, not at all. It's going to be fucking hard. It's going to hurt more than anyone could ever imagine. But you don't have to lose Tyson, Preach. You could still be a part of his life."

I release a heavy sigh. The anger that I have is still burning deep within me. "Right now, that's not goin' to happen," I say through gritted teeth. "I can't fuckin' do that."

"I get that. I doubt I could do that right now either. But give it time. Let time heal the wounds, and maybe one day you'll be able to."

I nod. "That's the only option there is."

He gives me a small smile. "Now, the real reason as to why I'm here..."

Now that's news to me. I assumed he was here to talk with me as the women are worried about me.

"The strip club is almost ready. From speaking with Pyro, I understand you're now taking charge of it."

I blink. "The fuck?" I knew this chapter had decided to go down the strip club route. It was voted on and passed in all chapters of the Fury Vipers as we hadn't done that yet. We hadn't sold women or even gone anywhere near talent at all. It needed to be voted on by all chapters. I didn't know it was almost ready to open.

His chuckle infuriates me. "Did he not share that with you?"

I don't answer. I recall a conversation that was had, but I was so fucking drunk, I can't remember much of it. Shit. I need to get the fuck off the booze and start living, but the alcohol is a balm to the pain I'm constantly in.

He gives me a knowing look and shares the location of the club. "The club needs a manager or two. You need to hire dancers and servers."

Fuck. "How the fuck am I supposed to do that?"

"My wife will be helping. Bars and clubs are her forte. You need to be present while hiring. Callie's waiting on you."

No fucking kidding. His wife is rich—beyond that even. She learned how to be a thriving billionaire from her father, who owns multiple hotels across the globe and is one of the richest men in the world. Together, father and daughter are unstoppable at anything they put their hands to. Having Callie helping us set up the strip club is the right move.

"Fuck, what time?"

"She's there at the moment and will probably be there all day as she's set up interviews for today. While I get that you'd rather not have to deal with this, my wife's taking time out of her day to do this."

"I won't disrespect your wife, Denis. Callie has helped this club out a lot. She deserves the respect of me going to the club and not leaving her to do all the shitty jobs."

Callie has gone out of her way to help the club. When Pyro and Chloe got together, Chloe let it be known that she didn't want to move away from her family. She'd been through a fucking lot, and she and her family have a close bond. That's something that every brother in the club understands because we have that bond with each other. But Pyro was tied. He couldn't abandon his club, yet he didn't want to lose the woman he loves, so Callie and Denis helped us. They organised things so that we didn't lose Pyro as a member and their daughter got to stay with the man she loves. They gave us a property that is now our clubhouse and have helped everyone get visas so we're able to stay in the country.

Without Callie and Denis' help, none of this would be possible. Because of them, I had a place to stay when I needed it. I was able to flee the States and come here, to a place where I'm able to find some solace. Not much, but a little. It's helped me understand that losing Tyson hasn't killed me. Fuck, it damn near almost did. But I'm here, alive, and I'm fucking surviving.

"I appreciate that, Preacher. You need anything, you just let us know."

I give him a chin lift. "I'll go to her now and get this shit sorted so that she's home to you tonight."

He laughs. "I'd appreciate that. See you later, Preach."

I watch as he walks away and I take a deep breath. I fucked up by not listening to Py when he told me what I had to do. I was so fucking drunk that I wasn't able to take it in. That can't happen again. I could have let the club down big time and that's not on anyone but me.

Once Denis leaves, I move to my bike and climb on. It's taken some getting used to—not driving on the right side of the road—but it's becoming natural now.

Living in Ireland is so fucking different to life in the States. New York is bustling and filled with high-rises and so many people. While Dublin is also filled with people, there's not a sense of urgency when traversing the streets. It's not as fast-paced and seems to be laid back. I'm not sure how I'm liking it. It makes for a good change, but I know my brothers and I will get restless. We'll want something to quell the chasing of the high that we seek. By the looks of things, there's nothing here that will do that.

I ride to the strip club and see that it's in a decent part of town. There's a sleek Bentley parked out front and I instantly know the vehicle belongs to Callie.

"Preacher," she says as I enter the club. She's got a bright smile on her face. The woman is fucking gorgeous. She's got an hourglass figure, and her hair is long and dyed silver. She's a real beauty, and the fact that she's one of the sweetest women you'll ever meet makes her that much fucking better. It's a shame she's married and the mother of a whole fucking football team.

"Callie," I say with a nod.

She gets up from the stool at the bar and walks over to me, her face bright with a huge, blinding smile. The second she reaches me, she opens her arms and hugs me. The woman's way too fucking nice, but that nice side of hers won't ever be tainted. Her husband and step-children, along with her own family, will never let anything happen to her. She's had her fair share of shit to deal with but she came out stronger than ever, and she did it with a smile on her face.

"Are you ready for this?" she asks, and I'm fucking relieved she's not mentioning Tyson. He seems to be the only thing anyone wants to talk about and I'd rather slit my fucking throat.

"Not really, but it needs to be done."

Her laughter is husky. "No wonder Chloe loves you. You say it how it is. I've already filtered out half of the applicants. You're opening a strip club, and you want this to be a success, so you want people who know how to hold down a job and who are also good at working with others. The last thing you want is people who can't do either."

"Ain't that the fuckin' truth. So, who are we startin' with?"

We walk toward the bar and I take a look around the club. It's as Denis said: ready to go. The poles are up, the booths are fitted, and there are tables scattered around the bar itself so the patrons can watch the show, kick back, and have a drink.

"Is there a back room?" I ask as I see two archways with curtains either side of the actual bar.

"Yes," Callie says as she points to the left hand side of the bar. "Through there is the back room. It's already monitored. We have cameras covering every position and there are no blind spots. We don't want the women or men to be put in a position where we're unable to help them."

I raise a brow. "Men?"

She grins. "Welcome to the twenty-first century, Preacher. Women love watching men strip. It'll bring you a whole new clientele. Have ladies nights with both men and women working the pole, and also have men working the back room on all nights too."

"Sounds good. So who's first on the list?" I ask, referring to the candidates coming in for an interview.

"First is Theresa. She's applying to be the manager of the dancers. She's had previous experience working in a strip club. She was a manager in a club in Manchester and has really good references. She's home as her father died, and she's living in his house. Once we're finished with the managerial interviews, we have the dancers and bar staff."

How the hell she managed to get all that information before she even interviewed anyone is beyond me, but I'm impressed.

"Okay, let's get this started," I say as I reach for the file Callie has for me and flip through it. She's gone all fucking out. Every applicant has a full dossier on them. "Do they know that they'll be working for the club?"

She nods. "Yes, everyone knows that." There's a little laughter in her voice. "Everyone knows everyone's business here. The news of the Fury Vipers coming to Dublin was huge. Add in the fact that you've opened a new custom build outlet and now a strip club, and you guys are making a big splash this side of the pond."

I chuckle. "Well, they should wait until we have one of our parties, then we'll definitely make a splash."

She shakes her head. "We won't be talking about that," she says. "I like you, Preach. I like the brothers, including Pyro. But I don't want to know what you all get up to, especially my daughter."

Her words make me laugh once again, and I realize it's the first time since I left New York that I'm not drowning in pain. Having to do this has taken my mind off Tyson, Reaper, and the entire mess. Instead,

I'm focusing on everything else that needs to be done in order to get this club up and running. I finally realize why Pyro gave me this job, and I should really thank him, but fuck, the guy's been on my ass since I arrived, checking in on me constantly, and while I appreciate the sentiment, it's been driving me crazy.

I hope there will be a time when the pain of losing my son doesn't try to cripple me. That there will be a time when I can think about Tyson without my heart ripping into pieces. Then again, hope so often leads to disappointment.

CHAPTER 3
AILBHE

FIVE MONTHS LATER

"Da," I sigh. "Come on, I really have to go to work. I can't be late." Not again. I've only just got this job. The last thing any of us need is for me to lose it. I'm the only one who's paying the bills. If I lose this job, then we're all fucked.

"Job," my da sneers. "Stripping isn't a job, it's a fucking abomination."

Oh, here we go again. My father has a problem with my job. I get it; not everyone is happy that I'm stripping. But it's the only job I could get that paid enough for me to pay the bills and make sure my family is taken care of. My da gets money from the government as he had an accident while at work. He hurt his back and hasn't been able to work since. But the money he gets is to keep his alcohol and gambling addiction up. My ma couldn't put up with it any longer and walked out. We haven't seen her for the past four months. So it's down to me to keep everyone from homelessness. It happened once, and I swore we'd never end up back there. Not again.

"Maybe if you didn't piss all your money away, then I wouldn't have to strip. But seeing as you're never going to change, Da, don't you dare try and make me feel bad for doing whatever it takes to keep this family fed and keep a roof over our heads."

He glares at me. The look of disdain on his face used to make me shiver in shame, but not anymore. "You're as bad as your ma. She was full of shit too."

I laugh, but it's mirthless and filled with spite. "You ran her away. She was sick of dealing with your bullshit, Da. Why on earth can't you see just how fucked up this is? I mean, I'm eighteen. I should be at college and living my life, but instead, I'm here, making sure Mikey, Fiona, Hannah, and Evie are safe and looked after. We both know you're not capable of doing that. So until you get your arse out of your head and stop acting like the martyr, when in fact you're the reason all of this shit has been happening, you don't get to try and make me feel guilty."

He reaches for his jacket. "Fuck you," he snaps and walks out of the house.

I take a deep breath and sigh. God, he's never going to change, and there's nothing I can do that will help change his perspective and get him to see that if he helped with the bills rather than spending his money on booze or gambling, things would be different.

Hell, it's so bad that he's started to steal my tips from my purse. On a good week, I make around two thousand euros, but we're in so much debt that I'm using the majority of my wages to pay that debt off, and then everything left over goes on food, heating, electricity, and making sure the kids have clothes that fit them. Having my da steal money from me just makes things so much harder. It's got to the point now that I sleep with my money on me so he can't steal it from us.

"Ailbhe," Mikey says as he shuffles into the room. "We'll be okay. You need to work."

I close my eyes. My brother is fourteen and he's the best person I know. He's not angry at me for taking this job. In fact, he's the only person who's actually supportive of me doing it. He's far from stupid. He knows how bad things are and he knows that if I don't do it, we'll be out on the streets.

"I don't have the money for a babysitter," I tell him

with tears in my eyes. "Da stole the money I saved up for it last week."

He nods. "That's okay," he promises me. "I called Ruairi."

I gasp as I turn to him. "You didn't," I whisper.

He glances away. "I'm sorry, Ailbhe, but I did. You can't do this alone. It's not fair. Ma should never have left. She should have kicked Da's arse out and made him leave. We all would have been better off had she done. Instead, she ran and left you to deal with everything. That's not okay. So I've called Ruairi."

I close my eyes. God, I'm going to have to deal with an overprotective brother now. Ruairi is away at college, or he was. He was in Cork and having the best time. He was thriving and living his best life. I was proud of him, and I was hoping that once I had paid off my da's debt, I could start to save money and give it to Ruairi to help with his expenses down in Cork, but that's now gone to shit. Ruairi's going to hit the roof when he finds out about everything that's been going on.

"When's he arriving?" I ask, wondering how much time I have before the shit hits the fan.

"He should be here soon. I called him this morning. He told me he would pack up his stuff and leave. I thought he'd be here by now."

I inwardly groan. This is not what I need. I've had

to put up with Da's shit for long enough, along with Ma's when she'd had enough of Da. I was always in the middle of it all, and now that she's gone, I'm right at the forefront, taking the brunt of it all. I don't know how much longer I'll be able to keep this up before I fall to pieces. It's hard. It's so fucking hard being in charge of so much and wondering if your hardest efforts will be enough. I understand why Ma left, but Mikey's right. She should have kicked Da's useless arse out of the house instead. We'd all be in a better place had she done.

"How much have you told him?" I ask.

His cheeks tinge with red, and I already know what he's going to say. "Everything. I've told him everything. He's mad at you, Ailbhe. Real mad."

I release a harsh breath. "I really don't care. I've done what I needed to do for this family."

Mikey nods. "I know. I've watched how hard you've worked, Ailbhe. And I know that you're also going to beauty school during the day and taking care of all of us while you're doing it. You've given up everything to help us."

I cross to him and pull him into my arms. "I'd do it all over again. I love you, Mikey. I love you, Hannah, Fiona, and Evie. I'll do whatever it takes to make sure we're all together and that you don't have to be without food or warmth."

His arms tighten around me and his body bucks, and I know he's trying to keep in his emotions. I hate that he's close to tears.

"It's going to be alright," I promise him.

"I know," he tells me. "You always make it good."

My heart clenches. God, he's the bomb. "Just keep up the good grades, okay?"

That's something that's changed since Ma left. Mikey's grades have drastically improved. I think it could be because I'm making him do his homework and I'm helping him out with the things he gets stuck with. I realized that our parents had been neglecting us, and in turn, we all neglected each other. I'm trying my hardest to ensure that everyone doesn't feel as though they don't matter. I want them to feel loved and cherished. So I'm giving everyone one-on-one time to ensure that they're okay, and since I've begun doing that, everyone has significantly improved. They all seem happier, and that's all I want.

"You're the best sister in the world. You know that, right?"

I give him a squeeze before releasing him. "I'm doing what anyone else would do. Now, have you finished your homework?"

It's seven in the evening, and Hannah and Evie are in bed, asleep. Fiona's lying in bed watching TV. She'll turn out her light at nine, and then Mikey will usually be fast asleep by the time I arrive home at around two-thirty in the morning.

"It's all done, as is Fiona's. While you were in the shower, I checked over it for her. She's doing really well."

I grin. "Just as you are. You're both the brains of the family. I hope Hannah and Evie take after you and not me."

He shakes his head. "You're crazy, you know that?"

The front door opens, and I turn and see Ruairi strolling in.

"Ailbhe," he greets me, but there's a slight bite to his tone. "Mikey."

"Ruairi, lovely to see you," I say with a sweet smile on my face. "But I'm in no mood to have an argument. I've already had enough shit off Da. I really don't need to hear from you too."

He sighs. "I wasn't going to argue with you, Al. I really wasn't. I've had a long fucking drive, and I had time to do a lot of thinking. I'm pissed. Christ, I'm fucking raging that you never told me how bad things had gotten. Had you done, I would have been able to help you. I would have been here so it wasn't you taking on the heavy burden of it all."

"But you were thriving, Ruairi. You were doing so well. I didn't want you to leave that behind. I'm doing okay. The kids are finally happy and they're doing better in school."

He nods. "Mikey's told me everything, Al. But it should have been you who did."

"You're right, I probably should have. But I did what I thought was best. Honestly, I truly believed I could handle it all. You're here now, which I'm really happy about. It's been a while since we've all seen you."

He grins and moves toward me, and just as I did to Mikey, he pulls me into his arms. God, it feels good to have him here, but I want him to finish his studies and live out his dream. Why should we both lose what we worked hard for? I may need help with the kids every so often, but I'm hoping that once I'm able to save up enough money, I can hire a babysitter to stay with them while I'm working.

"Go to work, Al. I'll be here to watch the kids."

I nod, relieved that I won't have to call work and tell them I can't make it tonight or even have Mikey take on the responsibility of looking after the other kids.

"Tomorrow, we'll talk," Ruairi says, and I smile. I should have known he wouldn't let me get away that easily.

"Tomorrow," I promise him. "Make sure Fiona's asleep by nine."

He raises his hand and waves me away. "We've got this."

"There's food in the fridge if you're hungry," I tell him as I reach for my duffle bag. "I'll be home later. Love you, bye," I shout as I leave the house.

The relief I feel knowing Ruairi is here is insurmountable. I hadn't realized just how much I needed someone here with me. As much as I'd like to pretend I'm okay, I'm far from it, but we're surviving and we're getting to a point where we're going to be okay. I'm not letting Da take the piss out of us and deprive the kids of what they need. I'm not letting him do as he pleases. If he wants to stay in the house, then he needs to behave.

"He's back," Tamara tells me with a wide grin on her face. Those gorgeous dimples of hers are deep as she smiles. "He's broody, but damn, that man is sexy as hell."

We're at the strip club, getting ready for the last set of the night. Tamara's a gorgeous, tall brunette. She's got big boobs and a big arse. She's one of the best people I know, and the greatest thing about her is, she doesn't give a crap about what people say or think about her.

I roll my eyes as I continue to brush my hair. There's no doubt in my mind that Preacher is sexy as sin, but Christ, the man is a complete fucking prick. He's such an arsehole, and it's the biggest turn off.

"It's busy tonight," I say, trying to change the subject. Every woman in this place loves the bikers. They bring a whole new dynamic to the city. The Americans are rugged, sexy, and dangerous. Hell, even the men who work here love them. They're different than the bikers we have here in Ireland. I can't put my finger on how they are; it's just the vibe that they give.

"Yep," Tamara says, popping the 'p'. "Everyone wants to gawk at the American hotties. It's a shame three of them are off-limits."

"Does anyone know who Raptor's woman is?" Kelsie asks as she joins us. She's short, but her height doesn't take away how beautiful she is. Her jet black hair flows down her back and is silky smooth.

We're almost finished. There's less than an hour until the club closes. It seems as though everyone decided to come out tonight. For a Thursday evening, the club is packed.

"Not yet," Tamara replies. "Whoever she is, she's a lucky lady. Then again, it seems as though Preacher has a lady too. The guy doesn't look at anyone."

Oh, how wrong she is. Preacher and I spent one night together weeks ago. It wasn't planned—hell, it was stupid. There was a party at the Fury Vipers Clubhouse and everyone from the strip club was invited. I went and got stupid drunk and ended up in bed with Preacher. It was without a doubt the best night of my life, but fuck, he was a complete arsehole once he'd finished. Since then, whenever I see him I pretend he doesn't exist, and it seems to piss him off.

I flip my head over and start to fluff up my hair. I'm back on stage again soon, and my feet are killing me. It's so damn busy tonight, I've done more private dances than any other night.

"You okay, Ailbhe?" Tamara asks. "You seem distracted today. Is it your da again?"

I sigh as I flip my head back and face Tamara. "He's an arse. Ruairi came home tonight after Mikey called him. He's angry that I didn't call him."

Tamara and Kelsie wrap their arms around me. God, I have the best friends ever. When I started working here, I was worried I wouldn't make friends. I'm a little awkward and don't make friends easily. But then I met Tamara, and we hit it off immediately. Kelsie started not long after we did, and it was as though the three of us had known each other for years. Our friendship is easy and we get along so well.

"He's home," Kelsie says. "It may not be what you want, but I think it's what you need. Let him help you, Al. You need someone to ease the burden."

She's right, I do, but I hate that he's sacrificing his education to do it.

"It's all going to be okay," Tamara promises me. "You've already shown you're more than capable of taking care of those kids. Never doubt just how amazing you are."

Tears spring to my eyes. Fuck, they're the best.

"No crying," Tamara says. "You've got to get out there."

She's right, I do. I shake my head and blink furiously to stop the tears from falling.

"That's it. Now go out there and put on the best performance of your life. It's a packed crowd, honey. You're going to make a fuck ton of money."

I laugh. She's right—the busier it is, the better the tips, especially at this time of night.

She slaps my arse and I can't help but giggle. These girls always know how to cheer me up.

An hour later and I'm exhausted. Not only have I been up on stage, but I've done seven private dances for the entire night. I earned nearly seven hundred euro tonight, which makes it my biggest night yet.

"Ready?" Kelsie asks as she links her arm through mine.

I nod. "Yep. Do you need a lift home?" I ask. She doesn't drive, and it's late. I'd rather she didn't walk home or even get a taxi at this time of night. Tamara's already gone, and as always, Kelsie and I are among the very last to leave.

"You're sweet," she says as we head for the exit. "But my dad's waiting outside."

"How is he taking you working here?"

She lifts her shoulders and shrugs. "Eh, not much he can say. Times are tough and you've gotta do what you've gotta do. I need money to go to college, and as I'm studying at Trinity, I'm able to live at home, which means I'm able to contribute to the household. That's taken a lot of stress off my parents."

"I wish my da was so understanding," I say with a sigh. "Mine just bitches about it."

"That's because he knows he's failing and that it's his fault you're here rather than doing what you always dreamed of."

Cold air hits us as we exit the building. Her da's car is idling at the curb. When she sees him, she grins at me. "I'll speak to you tomorrow. I want to know how you and Ruairi get on. It's been a while since you saw him last, Al. You know you've missed him."

"Yeah, I have," I admit softly.

"Go easy on him, yeah?" she says as she walks toward her da's car.

"I'll try," I reply, reaching for my keys and moving to my car.

"Who's Ruairi?" I hear a deep, baritone voice ask from behind me.

My pulse races and I can't help but release a squeak. "Christ on a fucking bike, Preacher, you can't go around scaring people like that," I hiss as I press a hand to my chest, feeling the thump of my heart. It's like I've run a marathon the way it's racing. I turn around and face him. Even though it's the middle of the night, I can still see him thanks to the moon shining brightly in the sky, along with the lights outside of the club. They illuminate him perfectly.

God, he's so damn handsome. Those dark brown, intense eyes of his; the ones that look as though they're searing through my soul and makes my heart race with just a glance. I scan his face, loving his beard and chiseled jaw. He's so fucking gorgeous. But as always, he ruins it all by opening his damn mouth. His brown hair is long and reaches his shoulders. I remember how soft it is. I ran my hands through it when we fucked. He's got tattoos that cover his arms, legs, and torso. The biggest one is the insignia of the motorcycle club he belongs to. The man is six-foot-six. He's a giant compared to my five-foot-seven. He makes me feel small, which is a feat in itself. His body is solid muscle, and it felt good to have his arms around me. But damn, he's an arsehole.

"You didn't answer my question. Who's the guy?"

I shake my head. "It's none of your business."

"That's where you're wrong. You work for me, and we don't need a jealous guy makin' problems."

Oh, he has some fucking nerve.

"Don't worry about my personal life, Preacher." I turn on my heel, but before I can take two steps away from him, his hand clamps around my wrist and he pulls me back. I land against his front, and he slides his arm around my stomach, holding me against him. I'm not stupid. I can feel the thickness of his cock against me. Been there and done that. I don't need a repeat.

"My cock was thrustin' inside you only weeks ago. You move on that quickly with everyone, babe?"

I wrench my arm away from him, and thankfully, he lets me go. "Go to hell. You're a fucking gobshite, Preacher. You're the one who treated me like shit, not the other way around. You don't get to act like the victim. I've done nothing wrong."

"That's where you're wrong. I haven't had my fill of you yet. I want more."

My lip curls in disgust. "Not going to happen. Find someone else to play with." I take a deep breath. I'm not going to argue with him. I want to go home, shower, and then crash. I have to get the kids up for school in less than five hours. I'll be lucky if I manage to get more than three hours of sleep tonight. "Goodnight, Preacher," I tell him with a little smile as I take a step backward.

"We're not finished here, nowhere fuckin' near."

I give him yet another smile. "Tell you what," I say as I continue to walk backward. I'm unable to take my eyes off him. The man's too bloody gorgeous for his own good. "If you can tell me my name, I'll consider talking with you. Until then, it's not happening. Goodnight."

This time, I turn away and walk toward my car. I can feel his heated gaze on my back as I climb into my small Toyota Yaris and start the engine. I glance in the rearview mirror and see Preacher is standing where I left him, watching me carefully.

Damn, that man seriously knows how to affect me. But I was right; he has no idea what my name is. He always calls me babe. I won't be treated like a whore. It happened once already, and that was one time too many. He has no idea that I was a virgin when we slept together, and I'm grateful he doesn't. We were both drunk, and I'm sure if he knew he took my V-card, there'd be some stupidity on his part and he'd think it meant a lot more to me than it actually did.

I drive away, noting he's still watching me. Once I've pulled out of the car park, I feel my body relax. I have a feeling that wasn't the last time I'll see Preacher.

CHAPTER 4
AILBHE

"Morning," I say as I watch everyone pile into the kitchen. Mikey looks well rested, which is great. Usually, he drags his feet when he comes to the kitchen first thing. "How are you all this morning?"

"How are you always so chirpy in the morning?" Fiona asks me with narrowed eyes as she slides onto the dining table chair. "Can I have tea and toast this morning?"

"Of course you can. Did you sleep well?" I ask as I hit the switch on the kettle.

"Yeah, but I wish we didn't have to get out of bed. Where's Da? He wasn't in his room this morning."

My heart breaks every time she tells me that. I can see the pain in her eyes. Whenever Da and I argue, he spends the entire night out doing God knows what. He sometimes doesn't come home for days. The girls adore Da, and they love spending the mornings talking with him. So whenever he's not here, I can't help but feel a little guilty, like it's somehow my fault that he's not here.

"He must have left early," I lie.

Her eyes flash with hurt before she closes them. When she looks at me again, the hurt is gone. I hate that she masks her pain. I don't want her to hide it from me. She should feel free to express how she feels, and if that means crying, then so be it.

"Did you girls see we had a guest last night?" Mikey asks with a grin.

I smile when both Hannah and Evie's eyes widen. "Who?" Hannah asks.

"Santa?" Evie questions. She's six, and she's really struggled with Ma leaving. She's dying for Christmas to come, and I have a feeling it's because she's going to ask for Ma to come home.

"Even better," Fiona replies. "Ruairi's home."

Both girls squeal. "Ruairi?"

"What's the shouting about?" the guy in question asks as he strolls into the kitchen. "Well, if it isn't my four favorite ladies."

I roll my eyes at his lack of charm. He's really laying it on thick with the girls.

Hannah and Evie jump to their feet and run over to

him. I turn back to getting the breakfast ready. The kids need to eat and get dressed so they can get to school on time.

"Evie, sweetie, what do you want for breakfast?" I ask, already knowing Hannah will want cereal. She never changes what she has, whereas Evie and Fiona love a mixture of things.

"Can I have toast too, please, Ailbhe."

"Sure thing. Tea too?"

She nods as she goes back to her seat.

"I'll have the same, thanks, Al," Ruairi says with a grin. "Do you need a hand?"

I shake my head. "Nah, I'm good. Mikey, what are you having?"

"Toast," he says. "I'll get the milk and jam out of the fridge."

"Oh, I want blackberry," Fiona tells him.

"I want strawberry," Evie cries. "Please?"

I love that she is always so polite. It doesn't matter who she's talking to, she will always say please and thank you.

"Ruairi?" Mikey asks.

"Christ, how many fucking jams do you have?"

"Fiona loves blackberry," I tell him. "Evie and I love strawberry, and Mikey loves raspberry. I think there's even marmalade around somewhere."

He raises a brow. "Domesticated, aren't we?"

"Someone has to be," I reply, unable to keep the bite out of my tone. I know he's just messing, but damn, it hit me deep. I didn't have a choice. For the sake of this family, I had to step up and look after everyone.

"I'll have strawberry too, Mikey," Ruairi says, not responding to my jab. "Has everyone got everything ready for school?"

The girls nod as I start to plate up the toast. It's Mikey who answers him. "All our homework is done. Ailbhe makes us sit at the table when we come home from school and do it before dinner. She helps if we need it. She also gets up before everyone to ensure our school lunches are ready."

Evie smiles as she nods. "She makes the best lunches ever. Everyone is jealous of my sandwiches, Ailbhe has shapes for me."

I laugh. She loves to see what shapes I make her. It's a game to see if she can guess what today's shapes are. She doesn't know that I bought new shape cutters the other day. They were on sale and I couldn't resist, not when I know how happy she is to have them.

I place everyone's breakfast on the table and start to make the tea and coffee, listening to them all talk. It's loud and chaotic, but everyone's smiling, and for me, that's all I could ever ask for.

I take a seat once everything is ready, and I'm

shocked when Evie climbs onto my lap and carries on eating as though nothing's happened.

"Are you okay, sweetie?"

She nods as she eats her toast.

I hold on to her and leave her where she is. She's comfortable and obviously needs the comfort.

"Are you working tonight?" Ruairi asks me.

"Yeah, I'm working all weekend. I'm off on Monday. How long are you here for?"

He glances around the table and sees that everyone is watching him, waiting for his answer. We've all missed him.

"Not sure yet. I'm here for a while," he replies and goes back to eating.

His answer was evasive, and I'm left wondering why he's not going back to college. Has something happened?

I glance up at the clock and see we've been eating and talking for a while. Everyone's finished eating. They've just got their drinks left. "Okay, kids, finish up your drinks. You need to wash up and get dressed."

"I don't feel well," Fiona says with a pout. I give her a look, and she sighs and gets to her feet, shuffling out of the kitchen with everyone following behind her. My sister is forgetting who she learned it all from. I hated school, but I hated my home life more. The arguments between my parents made me want to leave, so I revised like crazy to get the grades I needed to escape. I never expected to still be here, but I am, and I'm going to ensure the kids have a happy home.

"You've done great," Ruairi says once we're alone. "I don't remember a time when this house was filled with laughter and happiness." He scrubs his hand over his face. "Damn, our parents really fucked up, huh?"

"You have no idea. Once the kids go to school, I'll tell you everything that happened. But, Ruairi, what's happened with you? And please don't lie to me."

He grimaces. "I may have been kicked out of college."

I feel my eyes widen, and my jaw slackens. "How? When? Why?"

He chuckles, and it's low and without humor. "I fucked up. I got into too many fights for me to continue staying there. I've been working. I couldn't come home and say I failed."

"You didn't fail, you made a mistake. Did you like being in college?"

He shakes his head. "Fucking hated it, but I didn't want to stay here and listen to the constant fighting, or have to pick up Da when he was passed out drunk on the couch, or throw him into the shower because he pissed himself again."

I wince at the reminder of just how bad things can get with our da. "Yeah, not great times."

"How long has Ma been gone?"

"Almost six months now."

"Fuck. Has she been back?"

I shake my head. "Not once, nor has she called. I'm worried about Evie. She's been so nonchalant about it all, yet she's excited for Christmas. I do wonder if she's hoping Ma will return then."

"Honest to fuck, Al, from what I've seen since I got home last night, the kids are better off without both Ma and Da. You've made this house a home and it's obvious how happy the kids are. It's so fucking different than how we grew up."

I nod. "I didn't want them to have to live like that. I hated constantly walking on eggshells. It was fucking hell. But they really are happy and they seem to be thriving. It was weird at first, and they constantly asked where Ma was. I didn't know what to tell them so I said she had to go away for a while."

"You did the right thing, but you really should have called me, Al. I would have been home and helped you. I would have been able to help with the bills."

"About that," I sigh. "Da's in a lot of debt. I'm trying to pay it off, but he's just making things harder. He's been stealing my tips from my room. I wouldn't be surprised if he's stolen things from the kids and they haven't told me."

"He's always been a fucking prick," Ruairi grouses.

"When the fuck is he going to grow up? How is Mikey handling it all?"

"Better than I am, that's for sure. He's taking it all in his stride. He despises Ma, and he fucking hates Da. He's working his arse off, and I have a feeling it's so he can help me rather than do what he loves."

"Don't worry about that. I'm here now. You won't have to deal with Da's bullshit any longer. Mikey can relax and we'll figure out how to explain to the girls that Ma may never come back."

"I really don't want to see her if she does. She's caused everyone enough trouble as it is. Could you imagine if she returns and the girls all get their hopes up, only for her to dash them when she leaves again?" It's my biggest nightmare, and I'm not sure if there's anything I can do to stop it from happening.

"We'll sort it," he promises me.

I hear noise coming from upstairs, and I know the kids are ready. "We'll finish talking when the kids are gone," I tell him as I get to my feet and start picking up the dishes.

"Fiona, can you do Evie's hair for me?" I shout.

"Already done, Ailbhe. She's dressed and ready," Fiona shouts back. "Do you know where my Biology textbook is?" she asks when she comes downstairs.

I see that she did indeed do Evie's hair. My little sister is as cute as a button with her hair in pigtails. She looks so sweet, and she's got a smile on her face, as do Hannah and Mikey.

"It's in your school bag. I put it in there last night when you went to bed."

"You're the best," Fiona says, blowing out a breath. She must have thought she lost it. "Mikey's walking us all to school."

I shake my head. If he does that, he'll be late for school. "It's okay, I can do it."

"I got it," Mikey tells me, and I see the seriousness in his eyes. "It's just gym first lesson, so I can skip it."

"Is your arm still bothering you?" He hurt it a few weeks ago and hasn't done anything physical since. I'm not sure if it's because he hates the subject or if he's actually in pain.

He shrugs. "It's fine. You and Ruairi need to talk. Girls, get your bags and we'll go."

I cross to him and pull him into my arms. He doesn't resist—something he would have done months ago. Now, he's used to it and even hugs me back.

"Here," I tell him as I reach for my purse. I take out forty euros and pass it to him. "Get yourself something to eat on the way home." I know he doesn't tend to eat out unless there's extra money. "Go with your friends. Ruairi's here so you don't have to be home early."

Mikey grins. "I knew having him home would be the best. Are you sure?"

I nod. "Go. You haven't been able to hang with them for ages. Treat yourself."

"But the money—"

"Is fine. Honestly, it's okay. I had a really good night last night so I can afford to treat you. It's forty euro, Mikey, not a couple of hundred. So, please, enjoy yourself and don't worry."

He presses a kiss to my cheek, which shocks me. It's not something he's done before. "Thanks, Al. I'll see you later."

"Have a great day," I call out to Fiona and Hannah as they traipse toward the door.

"Bye, Ailbhe," Evie says as she rushes toward me. I crouch down and pull her into a big hug. "I'll miss you."

My heart melts at her words. "I'll miss you too, but I can't wait to hear all about your day when I pick you up, okay?"

She grins, giving me a nod. "Bye," she says as she follows her brother's lead and kisses my cheek.

"Bye, Evie. Have a good day."

She waves goodbye to Ruairi and runs up to Mikey. I watch as he takes her hand and carries her backpack for her.

"Mikey, can you—"

"Text you when they're at school safely. Yes, I can do that. Relax, Al, it's all going to be okay."

I blow him a kiss and feel my body start to relax once again. The stress is easing and I feel calmer. I'm so glad I have two amazing brothers who'll do anything to help.

"Okay," Ruairi says once the kids are gone. "Start talking. What happened? Ma's fucking nuts, Al. She's been dealing with Da's shit for years. What made her up and leave?"

I busy myself with washing the dishes as I talk. "That's just it, I have no idea. From the drunken rambles Da goes on, I've gathered that she found a new man and ran off to Cyprus with him. But I can't be sure."

"It makes no fucking sense. Why would she leave the kids behind?"

"That's it, I don't actually know. It's crazy. All I know is, the arguing ramped up. It got so much worse. They would have screaming matches at four in the morning loud enough to wake the house. It was beyond crazy. Then one night, Da was drunk as a skunk and began bitching about her being useless and not working, expecting him to take care of everything."

Ruairi scoffs. "Which is a goddamn fucking lie."

"Right?" I snap. "So I'm in the kitchen, cooking dinner, and the next thing I know, they're in the sitting room, screaming at one another. He's calling her a whore and she's calling him a drunken bastard." I shake my head. "I swear to God, Ruairi, I never saw it coming. He backhanded her so hard she fell to the ground."

Ruairi curses. "What happened next?"

"I told Da to stop it and screamed at him to back the fuck away. Of course, Mikey came downstairs at that stage. He must have heard me screaming. I told him to go back upstairs, and thank God I did because Ma then went for Da with the butcher's knife."

"The fuck?"

"Yeah. I managed to wrestle it off her, but she was raging—not that anyone could blame her. She was spitting mad, and that just started the two of them arguing again. And then she just looked at him and sighed. She told him she'd had enough and wanted out of the marriage."

"Let me guess, Da, being Da, told her to fuck off."

"Bingo. So Da went out, decided to get drunk again, and didn't come home for days. Whereas Ma went to her room, packed her bags, and left that night. Not one of them said a word. Hell, Ma never even said goodbye to the kids. She just upped and left."

"She should have tossed that cunt out on his arse. The fuck was she playing at just leaving? Fuck, had she called me, I'd have kicked the prick out of the house."

"Can't," I say. "I've tried, but he spouts shit about how it's his name on the lease and he'll have me arrested for trespassing. So right now, my hands are tied. I argue with him knowing he'll leave for days, but it's getting old real fast."

"No doubt. Fuck, we'll sort something out. Maybe we can find a new place? That way, we won't have to worry about him."

I sigh. I need to tell him everything. I turn and face him. "Yeah, about that... I can't."

His brows knit together. "What? Why?"

"Remember I was telling you that Da is in a lot of debt?" He nods. "Well, Da somehow managed to make me the one responsible to pay it back. He owes almost forty grand, Ruairi. I'm trying my fucking hardest to pay it off as much as I can, but every time I save up money, the bastard steals it."

"Why the hell are you paying it off and who the fuck does he owe?"

"Jed O'Connor," I tell him, and watch as he rears back. "I got it down to below thirty, but then Da borrowed more money from him, making it go back up. Jed's a prick. I tried to speak with Jed, to ask him to stop loaning da the money he told me he doesn't take his direction from me and that Da's the only Mangan he'll deal with. Which means I'm stuck, but paying this shit back."

"The hell you are," he snaps. "I'll go and see Jed, let him know it's not fucking happening."

"Don't," I hiss. "Don't."

His eyes narrow. "What the fuck aren't you telling me?"

I glance away, crossing my arms over my chest. "Da promised Jed that he could take me if I don't pay the debt back. When I first found out, I lost my fucking mind, Ruairi, but Jed and his men aren't to be messed with. Those bastards sent me to the hospital with a broken wrist."

Something I had to work through. Thankfully, my next door neighbor is a saint and was able to get me some heavy dose painkillers so I could work through the pain. It's healed, but it was painful for a while.

"I'll kill him, Ailbhe. I'll fucking kill him."

"I can't kick him out and I can't leave. No one is going to lease me a house while I'm paying off the debt, and I don't want Jed to come to the house, especially with the girls here."

"You leave Da to me. I'll start looking for a job and will help you out."

I close my eyes. "That would be great. Thank you."

He shakes his head. "Don't thank me, Ailbhe. I should have been doing this a fucking long time ago. No more secrets, okay?"

"I promise. No more secrets."

"Good. Now, first things first: changing the locks on the front door."

I laugh. Da has no idea what's about to happen. Ruairi and Da have always had a tumultuous relationship, and I have a feeling it's going to get a whole lot worse. I can't lie, I'm so fucking glad Mikey called Ruairi home. I'm not sure I'd have been able to be this relaxed had he not. I'm hoping that means things are looking up.

God, I pray that they are.

CHAPTER 5
PREACHER

"Who was the girl?" Raptor asks with a grin.

My brother came back from New York six weeks ago. He's settling in great, but he's determined to find his woman. The one he had a one-night stand with a while ago and hasn't seen since. Even Chloe hasn't seen her, and that's crazy seeing as Chloe is her best friend. The woman seems to have just vanished.

"What girl?" I ask, acting stupid. I know he saw me talking to the woman outside the strip club last night.

I fucked up with her. She was right; I have no idea what her name is. Hell, I can't remember much about being with her other than it was beyond fucking amazing, to the point I'm now dreaming about her. It's been weeks and she's all I've been dreaming about. It's beyond fucked up. But that's what happens when I hit the bottle. I become a fucking drunken asshole and I can't remember my own name, let alone anyone else's.

"You're full of shit, brother. You know that?" he says, shaking his head. "Never seen you chase tail before. What's with her anyway? She's not like your usual woman."

I don't answer him. Fuck, the woman in question is gorgeous, and I mean dead gorgeous. She's got a sweetness to her that I've only seen in the women my brothers have been with. She's intriguing, but I doubt she'll even give me the time of day. I fucked up, and it's going to take a whole lot of groveling to get her back. That's if I can remember her name.

"You at the club tonight?" I ask, hoping to change the subject.

"Yeah, and hopefully so are you. Wrath is hoping to stay with Hayley. James and Eva are sick and he doesn't want to leave Hayley with two sick kids."

"That's no problem. I don't mind going to the club."

Raptor chuckles. "I bet you fuckin' don't. Seriously, Preach, the woman is gorgeous, but are you sure you want to go down that route?"

I know what he's alluding to and I'm not sure if I should either. Losing Tyson was fucking hard. Having to deal with Pepper was a fucking headache, one I don't ever wish to repeat. Pepper was at the club for years. She was a club whore all the guys liked. But she changed once the brothers started to get old ladies. She became sneaky and set out to get pregnant in order to trap a brother in making her an old lady. Her jealousy drove her to make stupid mistakes. She thought I would be the perfect mark. Little did she know, I would end up being her worst fucking nightmare.

"Look, Preach, you want to go there, do it. Just be cautious, yeah?"

I nod. "It would help if I could remember her name."

His eyes widen before he bursts out laughing. "Holy fuck, you fucked her, didn't you?"

"Rap," I growl, not wanting him to even fucking go there.

He holds up his hands in surrender. "Right, I get it. She's yours."

No, she's fucking not.

"Brother, what are you going to do? You fucked her and didn't even know her name. No wonder she looked like she wanted to kill you last night."

I flip him the bird. "You're no fucking help."

"Look, it's easy. You just got to talk to Theresa. She'll know who you're talking about."

"That ain't ever happenin', brother," I say through

clenched teeth. I'm not going anywhere near Thersea, she's great an all, but she's fucking crazy. She was perfect for the managerial position.

He doesn't bother to hold in his laughter. "Oh, I forgot, that woman is crazy as fuck. I'll do it. She owes me a favor."

Crazy is right. Theresa is extremely protective of the women and ensures that nothing happens to them. Hell, she tries to keep everyone away from the dancers, especially the younger girls, like my red-haired beauty.

Raptor pulls out his cell and calls her. "Yo, Theresa, it's Raptor. I need a favor. The red-haired dancer, young, about twenty-ish... She was one of the last performers on the pole last night. What's her name?"

I wait with ill-concealed patience as he gets her name. I cross my arms over my chest as I watch him. The fuck is taking so fucking long? Is she giving him a run down of the entire dance staff? Fuck, I should have done what Callie wanted and interviewed all the dancers. That way, I wouldn't have to wait on anyone else to tell me the information I need.

"Thanks, Theresa, and don't worry, I promise you she's safe from me." He ends the call and turns to me, a stupid fucking grin on his face. "So your girl has an Irish name. From what Theresa said, it's pronounced Al-vah. Good luck trying to spell it. But also from what Theresa said, Al-vah is sweet and is one of the best dancers we have. She told me I'd better not run her off or she'll deal with me herself, and brother, I love you, but no one wants to deal with that bullshit."

Ain't that the truth. Theresa's like a fucking bulldog. There's no way she'll ever let anything happen to Alvah. But I have her name, and that's my way of talking to her.

"Thanks, brother. I'll see you tonight."

He flicks out his fingers in a salute as a way of saying goodbye. "Try not to forget her name again."

I flip him off. Fucking jackass. I may have been stupid by getting drunk the first time we got together, but it won't happen again. No fucking way.

Tonight, I'll be speaking with her again, and if everything goes according to plan, I should have her right where I want her. Back in my bed.

"You're back," she says with a wry smile. I've cornered her once again after work. Her hair's down and curled, her face clear of any makeup, and she's so fucking gorgeous. I have no doubt that she'd be gorgeous if she were in a trash bag.

"I am," I reply tersely. "You okay?" I ask, knowing that Raptor had to pull a guy off her earlier. I've never been drawn to a woman like I am her. I'm trying real hard to keep my distance, but there's a magnetic pull that's telling me I have to have her and I just can't keep away.

"I'm grand, yeah," she replies, her voice soft, that Irish lilt of hers sweet. My cock tightens at the sound. "It's nothing new, but thanks for checking on me."

"The fuck you mean it's nothin' new?" I growl, my anger spiking through me. "Does that shit happen a lot here?"

She sighs. "Look, men get drunk, they get loud, they get arrogant, they believe they're entitled to anything they want. So when we say no, they sometimes get a little handsy and demand we do as they want. It's fine, it gets dealt with."

I'll be ensuring that shit doesn't happen again. Fuck that. The dancers should be able to come to work and not have to be groped by assholes who can't take no for an answer.

I watch as she crosses her arms over her chest, pushing her breasts up further. Making me harder than before. "Did you figure out my name yet?"

"You tell me, Alvah?"

Her laughter is soft and lyrical. "Close. It's Ailbhe. A little less hard on the accent and you'll be grand."

"It's unusual. I don't think I've ever heard the name before."

She shrugs. "It's Irish. It means rock." She looks

thoughtful for a moment before smiling. "So you figured out my name. I'm intrigued about how you did it. I underestimated you, Preacher, and for that I'm sorry."

I grin. "Don't be, babe. I was an ass. I shouldn't have fucked you when we were both so drunk."

Her smile is blinding. "Welcome to Ireland. That happens on a weekly occasion. Don't worry about it."

I press closer to her. "You do that often?" I ask, hating the idea of her with any other guy.

"Nope. Don't worry, Preacher, you were the only one. I've got to go. I'll see you around."

Oh, fuck no. "You mean to tell me, I was the first?"

She releases a sigh. "Yeah. Don't worry about it though. It was one night."

Hell no. I'm in her face, my lips close to her own. "We're going to have a fuck of a lot more than one night."

She pulls in a ragged breath. "Preach—"

I silence her with my mouth. The kiss is hard and punishing. I slide my hand into her hair, tugging on it slightly, and she arches back, her lips parting in surprise. I deepen the kiss, sliding my tongue into her mouth.

Fuck, I'm rock fucking hard. There's something about Ailbhe that drives me fucking crazy, and I have a feeling she's going to get under my skin.

I pull back and see her lips are swollen, her eyes are wide, and she's breathing harshly.

"Preacher..." she says thickly. I fucking love the way she says my name with that sexy as fuck accent. She pauses as she looks at me, before she shakes her head and sighs. "I really have to go."

I grit my teeth as I release her. Fuck.

"I'll see you around, okay?" she says, almost as though it's the last time we're going to speak.

"Count on it, babe," I promise her.

She gifts me that gorgeous smile of hers. "Goodnight. Safe journey home."

Fucking sweet as fuck.

I press one last kiss to her lips and take a step back. "Night, babe."

I watch as she climbs into her car and starts the engine. One day, I'm going to be able to do something other than watch her walk away.

The redhead in the tiny black dress is fucking gorgeous. In a room filled with people, she stands out above them all. She's been smiling the entire night, and every person in here has taken notice of her. I've seen her in the strip club. She's a fucking huge hit with the men and women who come to watch her dance.

She's always been captivating, though we've never spoken. Hell, I don't think she's spoken to anyone other than the girls she's dancing with right now. But that doesn't mean she's not commanding attention. Her beauty does that the moment she's in your presence. But it's that bright fucking smile that makes her beauty magnify. Christ, she's out of this world beautiful, and tonight, she's going to be mine.

I down my glass of whiskey, loving the burn as it makes its way down my throat. I'm beyond drunk. It's the only way I can get through the night these days. Losing Tyson fucked me up, and I'm not sure there's a way I can recover. But booze and women sure do fucking help.

I get to my feet and make my way over to her. She's been giving me glances all night, so I know I'm not alone in this lust-filled craze I'm feeling.

"You give private dances, babe?" I ask, my lip against her ear as I slide my arms around her waist. When her ass hits my crotch and she continues to dance, I instantly get hard. Christ, this woman is going to be wild. I can tell.

"Sure," she says, her words a little slurred.

"Name's Preacher," I tell her.

She gives me a smile, one that lights up her entire face. "I know. I'm Ailbhe."

I take her hand and lead her through the throngs of people. Tomorrow is the one month mark of when the strip club opened, and it's been a fucking hit. It's brought in a lot more money than any of us predicted. Pyro wanted to celebrate, so he invited all the staff to come and party with us. Everyone turned up, and fuck, the clubhouse is filled with people having a good time.

Neither of us speak as I lead the redhead upstairs to my room. Her steps are a little unsteady, but I keep my arm on her and help her.

The moment we get into my room, I drag her against me, kissing her harshly as I unsnap my fly.

"Preacher," she groans as my cock springs free. Her eyes are filled with lust and a bit of fear as she looks down at my thick length.

"Gonna fuck you now, babe." I kiss her again, and this time, my hands roam her body. The tiny black dress barely covers her and is easy to slide off. When it drops to the floor, it pools between her feet. Her skin is creamy white and silky smooth. I caress her body, loving the way she feels against me. My cock is thick and hard—fuck, harder than it's been in a while.

She moans in the back of her throat as I run my hand along the outside of her panties. I don't hesitate; I pull at the hem, and it tears within seconds. She gasps as I push her onto the bed. I can't hold back any longer.

I position myself at her entrance, holding on to her thighs as I thrust deep inside of her. A low groan escapes me when her pussy tightens around my cock. Fuck, so fucking snug and tight.

She releases a strangled cry as I bottom out inside of her. The sound only spurs me on. I want to hear her cry out again and again. I fuck her hard and fast, unable to hold back. She's so fucking tight, I know it won't be long until I'm coming.

My thrusts are hard and fast as I grit my teeth and fuck her, twisting my hips to go deeper. She's whimpering as she claws at me, her nails digging into my forearms.

"Fuck yeah," I hiss, the pain from her nails adding to the passion. "I need you to come, babe," I say through clenched teeth. She's so fucking tight, I can't hold back any longer.

"Uggh," she cries out.

I continue to thrust, my balls tightening and my spine tingling. Christ, I can't hold it off. I quicken my pace, fucking her over and over again until I can't any longer. I thrust once more, before I still above her, groaning as I come.

The second I'm finished, I pull out of her, exhausted and about ready to pass out. I collapse on the bed beside her. "Thanks, babe. You can see yourself out."

I hear her swift intake of breath, followed by the rustling of sheets as she climbs off the bed, then the only sound I hear is her moving around the room, no doubt collecting her clothes.

I pass out before I hear the door close.

I wake with a start, sweat pouring from my body and my cock hard as stone. Fuck, I'm dreaming about that night again. It's been months since I've had her and she's always on my mind. This time, it was clearer than ever. No wonder Ailbhe fucking hates me.

I was an asshole.

Christ, I'm such a fucking dick.

I'm not sure if there's a way back from this.

CHAPTER 6
AILBHE

FOUR MONTHS LATER

'm woken by a loud banging noise. It sounds like someone's rummaging around downstairs.

"Want to calm down, old man?" Ruairi snaps.

I sit up in bed and rub my eyes. What the fuck?

"What the hell are you doing here?" I hear Da roar.

I glance at my phone and see it's not even seven in the morning. God, what on earth is going on? When the hell did Da get back? He's been gone for four months with not even a phone call. The day he walked out was the day Ruairi came home, and we've not seen him since.

"I could ask you the same question," Ruairi yells.

I jump out of bed, beyond pissed that they're having a screaming match at this time of the morning on a fucking Sunday.

"What the hell is going on?" I hiss. Thankfully, I'm able to keep my voice lower than these two amadans.

"What the fuck is he doing in my house?" Da snarls. "It's bad enough I have a whore living under my roof; I don't want to have a fucking waste of space too. Don't think I'll be paying for you to be here."

I snort. "It's not like you pay for anyone, Da. I'm the one paying the bills."

"You've got an attitude problem, girl, and I don't fucking like it. You'd best watch who you're fucking talking to. Have some fucking respect."

I roll my eyes. Oh, here we go again. Da loves to lord about the place. He believes that because he's older than I am, he's better than me.

"I lost respect for you the day you hit Ma. Not to mention, you left your eighteen-year-old daughter to pick up the pieces of your heartbroken children after Ma left. Oh, and I'm also paying off the debt you've racked up and I'm covering all the goddamn bills. So no, I won't have respect and I don't care who the hell I'm talking to. What are you doing here?"

His eyes flash with anger and his nostrils flare. "I'm warning you, Ailbhe, don't fucking test me. You'll not like the consequences."

The bitter laugh that escapes me is something that I know will rile him up, but I can't help it. The man's ridiculous. How does he truly believe that I'll do whatever the hell he tells me to do? "What are you going to do, Da? Steal more money from me? You've really sunk to a new low, haven't you? Stealing money from your child, money that keeps a roof over your children's heads."

"That money is dirty money," he snarls. "Money that you've whored yourself out for."

I raise a brow. I'm not going to let him make me feel guilty for doing something he forced me into. I won't be made out to be a whore when I'm doing right by my family—something that he himself should be doing. "Jealous?" I taunt, knowing that he's envious of the money that I'm making. Hell, he's resentful that I have a better relationship with the kids than he does. He never took the time to get to know them. He never took the time to get to know me.

His face reddens. "Don't," he says, his voice vibrating with anger. "Don't fucking push me."

"Best you leave," Ruairi says, stepping in front of me, trying to shield me from Da's view.

"Best get out of my way, son. You wouldn't want Ailbhe here to find out the real reason you're home, would you?"

I glance at my brother, wondering what the hell

Da's talking about. Ruairi doesn't look at me. In fact, he pushes closer to Da.

"Try it," he snarls as he squares up to Da. "Try it, old man, and see how far it gets you."

Da laughs. "He's just as bad as I am, Ailbhe. He's been gambling his money away. The fighting he's been doing? Illegal bare knuckle boxing. And he's been betting on his fights. He's lucky he's not in prison."

My body trembles as I watch Ruairi's eyes narrow. He's not denying what Da's saying, which means it's true. Fuck, what the hell is going on? Why would he do that? He knows how bad things have gotten with Da's gambling. Even before he left he knew how bad Da was, so why on earth would he do it?

"You're done," Ruairi hisses. "Time for you to fucking leave."

"This is my house, boy. You're not going to evict me from my own home. You can't. I'm the tenant on the lease."

"You haven't made a payment on the rent in over six years, Da. Ma did, and now Ailbhe does. I've spoken to the landlord and he's agreed to put the tenancy in Ailbhe's name. Your lease ended yesterday."

What?

Da fumbles in his pocket. He pulls out his phone and quickly hits dial on a number before bringing it to his ear. "John? Yeah, it's me, Peter. What's this shit about the lease ending?"

I watch on, unable to breathe as Da's face gets redder with each passing moment.

"You can't fucking do this to me, John. You hear me? You can't do this."

I'm dumbstruck as I watch on. How on earth did Ruairi manage to do this? When did he have the time?

Da edges closer to us, and I skirt around Ruairi and try to position myself between them. The last thing I need is them fighting.

"You arsehole, Ruairi. The fuck do you think you're playing at?"

Ruairi smirks. "Maybe now you'll realize just how much of a fucking screw up you truly are. You're useless, Da. You're fucking useless. You can't take care of your family, you piss away your money, and then you have the nerve to steal from your daughter—the woman who's keeping a roof over yours and your children's heads. Did you think making her pay your debt was going to have no consequences for you?" Ruairi shakes his head. "No fucking way. If I have to go fucking see Jed O'Connor myself, so be it, but I swear to fucking God, Ailbhe won't be paying it off any longer."

Da's enraged. I don't think I've seen him so angry before. His eyes are shining with unshed tears, the vein on his forehead is bigger than ever, and his jaw is clenched. I catch a glimpse of his hand. It's balled up into a fist.

"Don't," I say as I step in front of Ruairi. "Da, don't do it. The girls are upstairs. They don't need to see you two fighting," I say as I raise my hands in front of me, but it's too late.

Da pulls back and lets his fist fly, hitting Ruairi, which only infuriates my brother and causes him to fight back. I'm stuck between two grown men fighting, and no matter how much I beg for them to stop, they continue to throw punches at one another.

"For the love of God, will you two cop the hell on and grow the fuck up?" I snap as I push against both Da and Ruairi's chests. I have one hand on each and I'm pushing as hard as I can, but neither man moves. They're both angry and not listening to me.

"Move, Al," Ruairi growls as he once again throws a punch at Da.

I'm so angry that neither of them are even considering that the girls could come downstairs at any moment and see them acting like gobshites. I drop my hands from them and turn to walk away. If they're determined to pound each other into the ground, then fuck them. They can get on with it.

Before I'm able to escape the fray, a stray fist lands against my temple. The sheer force behind the blow knocks me off my feet, and I crumple to the ground. My vision blurs, and the last thing I hear is Mikey calling out my name.

"The fuck do you think you were playing at?" Ruairi hisses at me a while later.

I roll my eyes as he continues to pace the room. I passed out, and when I came to, Ruairi was doing just as he is now and pacing the room, whereas Mikey was trying to wake me up while applying a cold compress to my head. Da left not long after I passed out. Not that I'm surprised. He's usually gone at the first sign of trouble.

The girls woke up during the commotion, but thankfully, by the time they came downstairs, I had regained consciousness. The girls are far from stupid, though. They know something happened. They're watching us with wide eyes as they eat breakfast.

"Seriously, Ailbhe, you could have been really hurt," Mikey tells me, a slight tremor in his voice. "Watching you go down without a sound..." He shakes his head, his voice cracking at the end. "Don't do it again."

"I didn't mean to," I whisper, hating that he's so upset. "I just didn't want them fighting. I didn't want the girls to come downstairs and see it happening."

Ruairi sighs. "I was an arsehole. I baited him and pushed him to it. I'm sorry."

I shake my head and wince as pain lances through my temple. "It's fine," I say, still uneasy but feeling a little better. I know that once we're alone, Ruairi and I are going to have a conversation. He's left a fucking lot out about why he's home. I despise lies and he damn well knows that. He should have been upfront with me from the start. I would have been pissed, but I would have gotten over it. Finding out that he lied to me just makes me sad.

"I'm okay," I assure them. "I'm going to have a sore head for a while, but I'm good."

Ruairi's eyes narrow, makes me wonder whether he can see through the lie, but Mikey nods, looking relieved. "I'll take the girls to the park once they're finished with their breakfast; give you some time to rest. Please don't get between them again. They're capable of fighting amongst themselves."

I bring my finger to my heart and make a cross. "Promise."

He gives me a big smile, looking a lot more relaxed than moments ago. "Good." He turns to the girls. "If you're finished, shall we go to the park?"

Fiona's eyes narrow but she nods. I have a feeling she'll spend the entire time trying to get information out of Mikey.

The girls all get to their feet, and I'm shocked when every single one of them brings their plates and cups to the sink. Usually, they'll leave them on the table for me to clear.

Twenty minutes later Ruairi and I are sitting at the table. He looks contrite, unable to look me in the eye, and I know it's because he lied, but I need answers from him. I need to know why he lied.

"I knew you'd be angry that I was fighting for money. I knew you'd be raging that I was gambling, especially with everything Da's put us through."

"I would have been, yeah, but I would have gotten over it. God, Ruairi, you didn't have to lie to me. I may not have been happy, but we'd have sorted it out."

He runs his hand over his face. "I know. I fucked up. I'm sorry."

"So what happened with the landlord? How did you manage to get him to change the tenancy over to me?" I ask, still unsure about how that actually played out.

His grin is cunning and I can't help but smile. "I went to see John. He hasn't changed much, has he?"

I laugh. "You mean he's still a miserable old bastard? No, he hasn't."

"I told him that you'd been paying the bills for the past few months and that Ma had gone. To say he was displeased is an understatement. So it was easy for me to ask him to change the tenancy over to you. He said Da's a useless bastard and that if you're paying the bills, at least he knows he'll get the money."

I nod in agreement. I always pay the bills on time. I'll do whatever I can to ensure I have payment, including not having food myself. "So, Da's not going to be able to hold that over me again?"

He shakes his head. "Nope. No more."

I sigh with relief. "Thank God. He's been saying that at least three times a week before you got here. So he's gone. Did he even say anything before he left?"

"Nope. Just the usual bullshit of being disrespected in his house and how he's the man of the house and should be given the respect he deserves."

My lip curls in disgust. "He should learn that respect is earned, not demanded. It pisses me off that he doesn't give a fuck about the kids."

"Him nor Ma. What the hell are they thinking?" He shakes his head. "I called her, you know?"

I blink, surprised by his words. "You did?" I ask, wondering if she answered him or if she's been ignoring him like she does me and the others.

"She answered, acting as though nothing's happened. She was cheery, Al, fucking cheerful as could be."

"Lovely," I reply dryly.

"That facade obviously changed when I questioned

her about her whereabouts. Imagine her surprise when I told her I was at home with the kids and she was nowhere to be seen."

I'm not surprised she tried to play it off. Ruairi was always her favorite and she never hid that from anyone.

"You were right. She's got a new fella and they're living it up right now. From what I gather, they're in England. She told me she won't be back and that she's finally looking after herself. Whatever the fuck that means."

I sigh. "How the hell am I supposed to tell the girls? It's going to break them."

He nods in agreement. "All we can do is be honest with them. They're not stupid, Al, you've said so yourself. The girls are smart and they know something's been going on. So we need to let them know. We can keep out the shit they don't need to know, but they do deserve to have some information."

I groan. "That's going to be a great conversation to be had."

"I'll have it with them. You're working tonight. While you're at work, I'll tell them all. What do we tell Evie?"

I glance away as tears spring to my eyes. "She needs to know," I whisper, hating that we're going to break a six-year-old girl's heart. "They need to know about both Ma and Da. I don't want them holding out hope that either of them are going to change. We did that for long enough. I want them to have a happy childhood, Ruairi. I don't want them to lie awake at night wondering if tonight's the night Da will be home and sober for once. It's not the way I want any of them to live."

It wrecked me by believing the lie that my parents sold me. It rocked to me to the core to find out just how fucked up our family life was and I never want to put my siblings through that. They're content right now with how things are, but I know they're going to ask questions and the truth could send them spiraling. They've dealt with the bullshit from our parents long enough. No more. I don't want them to be hurt again.

CHAPTER 7
PREACHER

"Yo, Preach," Py says as he enters the club office.

I've spent the majority of the day finishing off beefing up security here. After learning that more than a few men have been handsy with the dancers, I put a stop to it. It's been four months and we're almost finished with the upgrades to the security.

I raise my head from the computer and look at him. He's fucking happy. I never thought I'd see my brother look so in love, but he is, and I'm happy for him. He's changed a lot since meeting Chloe. He even got new teeth, replacing the ones that had been knocked out due to fighting. He still looks dangerous, like he'd kill you with one hand—something he can and has done—but he's not as rough around the edges.

"Your girl... everythin' okay there?" he asks.

Raptor repeated everything he saw go down between Ailbhe and I the night we were talking outside the club. But he didn't just tell one person. No, the motherfucker told the entire club.

"What'cha mean?" I ask as I stare at him.

"Have you seen her today?" he questions, and I shake my head. "Then I advise you to go and do that. Brother, brace yourself."

Fuck.

I get to my feet, worry coursing through me. My steps are heavy and filled with purpose as I prowl through the club. I scan the area and see she's just finished up a lap dance. Knowing that some guy is getting turned on by her, pisses me off, but she's not mine, and there's nothing I can do to stop her.

It's been four months and I've kept my distance. The woman deserves a lot better than someone who's as fucked up as I am. But that doesn't mean I haven't been watching her. Even though I'm keeping away, I always find that I'm drawn to her.

I cross the room to her and immediately know what Pyro was talking about. She's done a shit job of hiding the bruise that's forming on her temple, not to mention there's a cut on it.

I grab her arm and pull her away from prying eyes. "The fuck happened?" I growl.

She wrenches her arm away from me. "What the hell are you playing at?" she hisses. "God, Preacher, this is my workplace. You can't do this."

I ignore the anger in her voice, but I do note that her being angry is something to behold. "Tell me what the fuck happened."

She gives me a blank stare, and instead of answering me, she crosses her arms over her chest and raises her brow.

"I can see the bruise. If you don't want me to go nuclear, tell me who the fuck hurt you."

"I walked into a door," she says, and I can see that she's lying. She's a lousy liar, which is good information to have in my back pocket. "I'm clumsy like that."

"Why are you lying?" I hiss as I push closer to her. "Tell me who hurt you."

"Why do you care?" she snaps. "Seriously, Preacher, why the fuck do you give a shit about me? I don't understand the stupid game you're playing. One minute you're all over me and can't get enough of me. You fuck me, and then you kick me out of your room without letting me catch my breath. Hell, you didn't say a single fucking thing to me after that night, then you're all up in my shit, wanting to fuck me again. Then you hide, it's been four months since we last spoke. So tell me, what the fuck are you playing?"

The way her eyes flash with anger and her cheeks

tinge with pink... Fuck, she's so fucking gorgeous. "I'm beyond fucked up, babe. I'm so fucked up, I drink to block out the pain. You want to know what I'm playin' at? You're the only thing I can fuckin' think of. You're all that I see. You've wrecked my brain and I can't escape. I have no fuckin' idea what the hell is goin' on. All I do know is that you're hurt and someone laid their hands on you, and I want to track them down and kill them for doing so. No one touches you."

She laughs. "You're crazy, you know that? Certifiably crazy."

I shrug. "That may be so, but you haven't answered my question, Ailbhe. Who hurt you?"

She shakes her head. "Don't worry about it, okay?"

"That's not goin' to work for me. You think I'm crazy, babe? You haven't seen anythin' yet. So I'll repeat: who hit you?"

She releases a heavy sigh. "My da, okay? He and my brother were fighting and I tried to stop it. He hit me by mistake, and I've got a lovely bruise and a banging fucking headache as a souvenir. Now you know, so can I please go back to work?"

She's feisty tonight and I fucking love that. "Why are you workin' if you're sick?"

Her lip curls as she taps her foot impatiently. "Not all of us have money to throw around willy nilly, Preacher. Some of us have people who rely on us and need this job to keep a roof over their heads. So I can't just call in sick because I have a headache."

I run my thumb over her lip, loving the way she pulls in a ragged breath. "You need money, babe? I can give you some."

She glares at me and takes a step back. "Just because I work here, that doesn't make me a whore, Preacher. I don't need your money. Why don't you shove it up your hole and fuck off."

I stand rooted to the spot as she gives me the filthiest look I've ever seen before flipping her hair over her shoulder and walking away.

What the fuck just happened? I'm not entirely sure how the conversation turned to her telling me to fuck off.

"Brother," I hear Pyro say from behind me. "I don't think I've ever seen someone put you in your place so eloquently before. What the hell did you do to that woman to make her so infuriated with you?"

"I have no fuckin' idea," I growl. But I fully intend to find out.

I spend the entire night watching her, making sure she's okay. I also keep an eye out for any guy getting a little too close for comfort. She's been hurt enough today as it is. She doesn't need to deal with any more assholes.

I need to find out what the fuck the deal is with her

father. The anger that flashed through her eyes at the mention of him makes me wonder what he's done to her.

"You're an arsehole, you know that?" I hear a quiet voice to the left of me say.

I glance over my shoulder quickly and grit my teeth when I realize it's Theresa. No doubt the woman's here to warn me off Ailbhe. She seems to have appointed herself their mom, which is great—as long as she doesn't get in my way.

"I do, in fact, know that," I tell her. It's no fucking secret that I'm a bastard. Hell, I killed a woman with my bare hands, something I never thought possible. But fuck, Pepper deserved every single thing I did to her. Fuck, she deserved a whole lot fucking more. She got away lightly in my eyes.

Theresa releases a stunned laugh. "I didn't expect you to say that."

"Not been around bikers much, have you?" We know who we are and what we are. All of us are assholes on any given day. There's no doubt about that.

"No, but you aren't as bad as your reputation says you are."

I bark out a laugh. "Oh lady, you have no fuckin' idea who we truly are."

She nods. "That may be true, but the way you've all

been looking out for the dancers shows that you actually care. Many don't."

"Working for the Fury Vipers puts you under our protection," I state simply. It's fucked up if we allow anything to happen to anyone under our protection.

"What about Ailbhe? That looked like a lot more than her just working for you."

"That's a fucked up situation all round. I have no idea what's going to happen."

"She's going through a lot," she tells me. "Her brother, Ruairi, is home, and from what I can gather, things at home aren't all they seem."

My gut tightens at her words. The response in itself is telling. Ailbhe has gotten herself deep under my skin. I'm feeling things I shouldn't be. I'm beyond fucked up, and a woman like Ailbhe... she's sweet, smart, and gorgeous. My baggage would drown her, just as it is me. My past is who I am. It's marked me in more ways than one.

Ailbhe deserves someone who's able to give her everything, and that someone ain't me. But the thought of her with someone else makes me want to find them and tear their heads off their bodies.

I run my hands through my hair. Christ, I'm losing my damn mind. What the fuck is wrong with me?

The club is closed and the dancers are leaving. The moment they step outside the club, they're making a mad dash for their vehicles. It's raining, something that happens often here, and the dancers are getting soaked as they rush toward their cars.

"Goodnight, Tamara," I hear Ailbhe say. "I'll see you tomorrow."

Ailbhe has a tight-knit group of girls she's close to. Both of whom seem to know about her hatred of me. I get that I fucked up with her, and I don't know if there's a way to get her to forgive me.

The girls step outside, both of them grinning at one another. "Night, Al, see you tomorrow. Tell that hunk of a brother of yours that I can't wait to meet him."

I hear Ailbhe retch. "Never going to happen. Ruairi is a gobshite, Tam. You're better than that."

Tamara dramatically sighs. "Why can't I find a decent guy?"

Ailbhe glances at me, her eyes gazing over me from top to bottom. "Don't ask me. I can't either."

I grit my teeth. I fucking hate the thought of her being with anyone else. If I find out that she's been with anyone, I'll probably kill them. I'm that fucking unhinged when it comes to her.

Tamara giggles. "Gotta go. Talk to you later."

"What do you want, Preacher?" Ailbhe asks once Tamara's in her car. "And don't lie to me, okay? I know you're standing out here for a reason. Usually, you'll be gone by now. So what gives?"

I grin. "Keepin' tabs on me, babe?"

She rolls her eyes. "You didn't answer my question."

"I wanted to talk to you."

She sighs. "Really?" she asks, as though it's the last thing she wants.

"Yeah, really. What's with the attitude?"

She laughs. "Seriously?" she asks incredulously. "You truly have no idea, do you?"

I cross my arms over my chest and watch her. I don't give a fuck that we're both getting wet from the rain. I want answers.

"You fucked me and then was a complete bastard. I get it. It's who you are. And I was fine with that, especially as you left me alone. Then you're suddenly sniffing around me, kissing me, and then you disappear. You're giving me whiplash."

"I told you, babe, I'm completely fucked up. I can't function anymore. I'm beyond wrecked. Tell me, do you think you could handle me?"

She stares at me, her eyes narrowed. "Did I say I wanted to? No. I just don't want to be part of this weird, fucked up game you're playing. I have emotions, Preacher, and I know you don't give a fuck about them, but I do. So stop toying with me."

"You're the one who has no idea," I snap. "You've

gotten into my fuckin' head. You've dug yourself so deep in me that you're all I fuckin' see."

Her lips part and she takes a step back.

"I'm fucked up, Ailbhe, completely and utterly fucked up. You deserve so much better than what I can offer you. I try... I fuckin' try to stay the fuck away, but I can't. I'm so drawn to you that I can't keep away."

"Preacher," she whispers. "What happened?"

I shake my head. "Not talkin' about it." Fuck, I doubt there's ever going to be a time when I'll want to talk about what happened with Tyson or even with my past.

"I don't know what to say," she says, still whispering.

"Nothin' to say," I tell her. "I'm all for us fuckin', but that's all I can give you."

I might as well be honest with her. It's a little crass with how I've worded things, but I'm upfront.

She sighs. "I don't have time for anything. Hell, I barely get enough sleep as it is."

"Fuckin', babe—that's all it is."

She glances around the parking lot, and I note that her car and my bike are all that's left. Theresa locked up and left while we were talking.

"Where?" she asks, bringing her hands to her hips. "I'm not bringing you home and there's no way you're bringing me back to the clubhouse, so where do you propose we fuck?"

I grin. "You wanna fuck, babe?" I ask and watch as she squirms. "Then that's exactly what we'll do."

I reach for her, bringing her closer to me. The moment I have her in my arms, I slant my lips down against hers. It's been too fucking long since I've had her. I've been waiting for the moment I could have her again.

I spin us around and walk her backwards. There's a dark alleyway at the side of the club that I know doesn't have any security cameras. The rest of the club and parking lot is covered, except this part. The alleyway is dimly lit. There's just enough light so that I can see her.

I press her against the wall as I continue to kiss her. It's frantic, and she's groaning as she grinds against my thickening cock. I reach between us and unbutton my fly, freeing my thick length, as she shimmies out of her panties and leggings.

I lift her up, and her legs circle my waist as we continue to kiss. I position my cock at her entrance and groan low in the back of my throat as I sink into her.

"Oh, Preacher," she whines as I enter her.

I can't hold back. I pull out, leaving just the tip of my cock inside of her, and then I slam back into her. I've lost the last threads of my control. The only thing I can think of is fucking her, getting as deep as possible inside of her, making up for lost time. Months I've been without her, months I've dreamed of her, and yet nothing feels as good as being inside of her.

Christ, she's so fucking tight.

"Ailbhe," I groan as I keep up the relentless pace. She's mewling like a kitten with every stroke.

Neither of us give a fuck that the rain is pouring down on us, or that we're both soaked through. All I care about right in this moment is being with Ailbhe.

"I need to come," she gasps, her arms tightening around my neck as she pushes down on my cock.

"Not yet," I growl. If she comes now, it's going to push me over the edge, and I don't want that, not right fucking now.

"Please," she begs as her pussy contracts around my cock.

"Fuck!" I snarl. I fuck her harder, and the tingling begins and my balls tighten. "Fuck, Ailbhe," I growl. "Fuck, fuck, fuck," I hiss as I piston into her like a man fucking possessed. "Come for me, babe. Come now," I snarl.

Her body tightens, her back bows, and her breath hitches. She screams out my name as her pussy convulses around my cock. I continue to thrust into her, once—twice—thrice, before I bury myself to the hilt and come.

"Christ," I grunt. "You make me lose my damn mind."

Her laughter is soft and lyrical as I pull her off my softening cock and help her to her feet.

"Sounds about right," she says, and releases a yawn as she quickly gets dressed, pulling on her panties and leggings. "I need to get home."

I nod as I step backward, buttoning my fly while I watch her. I have no idea why I'm pissed she's leaving. This is exactly what I wanted. No strings. Just sex. So her saying she's going home should make me happy, relieved even. But she seems happy to leave.

I walk her to her car. She's smiling as she slides into her seat. "I'll see you soon, Preacher."

I lean down and press a kiss to her lips. "Count on it, babe." I close the door and take a step back. She starts the engine and pulls out of the parking lot. I watch as the vehicle disappears, and I can't help but wonder why I'm so fucking attached to her. I don't even know her. Fuck, I don't trust anyone but my brothers. I doubt I could ever put my trust in a woman again, not after the shit that went down with Pepper.

That bitch fucked up my life. She got away easy with the shit she did. She'll burn in Hell, that's for sure.

CHAPTER 8
PREACHER

"You good, brother?" Pyro asks as he takes a seat beside me. I bring my beer bottle to my lips as I glance around the clubhouse. Denis and Callie's kids are here as Callie wanted to spend time with her daughter while Denis was working. She has all four children with her. There's also Wrath and Hayley's kids—Eva and their nine-month-old, James. It's getting easier to be around the kids, but fuck, it still brings back a fuck ton of memories. I miss Tyson so fucking much, and as much as I'd hoped the distance between us would ease that, fuck, it hasn't.

"You still not sleepin'?" he asks and I sigh. He sees everything. The man knows what's going on with everyone. There's not a day that goes by that one of my brothers doesn't ask how I am. I get that they're looking out for me, but it's not what I need. It's just bringing up my past, and Christ, that is the last thing I fucking need. I may be struggling, but there are times when I'm able to push through it, but then they'll ask questions, which'll send me spiraling and make me want to drink. Hence why I'm having a fucking beer before it's even mid-afternoon.

I don't answer him. I don't want to talk about it and I sure as hell don't want to relive it all.

"You've always been a stubborn fuck," Py spits. "We're just worried about you."

"Get that," I say as I take another sip. "But you've gotta understand, brother, it happened, and there's nothin' I could have done differently. I'm tryin' to fuckin' move on, but constantly bein' questioned ain't fuckin' helpin'."

I hear his deep intake of breath and watch as he nods. "We're goin' about this the wrong way." He glances over to where his old lady is sitting. She's smiling brightly as she talks with her mom while they watch the kids. His woman's happy, and I know that's all Pyro's ever wanted. Moving to Ireland was the only option the man had to ensure that he kept the woman he loved. While he lost being around his brothers, he gained a fuck of a lot more. His relationship with his sister, Hayley, strengthened, and in turn he's closer to his niece and nephew. I don't think I've ever seen my brother as happy or as settled as he is here.

"We'll do better. But, brother, the drinkin' has to stop."

"The fuck?" I snarl as I glare at him.

"I remember how shit was when Reaper was sent down; how you turned to alcohol to get rid of the guilt. You use booze as a way to numb everythin'. I won't let you sink that low again."

"Don't need to numb shit," I lie. "I have a drink when I want to, not 'cause I need to."

I've felt a lot of guilt in my life. What went down with Abel, it was beyond fucked up. Thankfully, before I spiraled too deep, I found the club, and I was able to move past the guilt. But then Reaper took the blame for my fuck up. I knew the guy was waiting for me outside the club and I knew he was going to provoke me. I should have walked away, but fuck, I didn't. Instead, I beat the ever-loving shit out of him and almost killed him. The cunt called the cops beforehand in an attempt to set me up, and boy did he do it good. Only, Reaper was there, and he took the fall for me. He served four years in prison for me, ensuring that I didn't serve a life sentence. Christ, that guilt ate me up. I felt it deeply. For four fucking years, I couldn't function. The knowledge that my brother was inside for a crime I committed was more than enough to send me spiraling. I was in a bad way. Then I found out that my son wasn't mine, but Reaper's. I couldn't keep Tyson from him. The man had already given so fucking much for me. I couldn't keep his son.

Now, my life's in fucking shambles. Its guilt and pain that threaten to knock me to my knees every fucking time I open my eyes, every time I breathe. It's fucked up that I can't seem to escape it. Nothing I do is making it easy.

He gives me a sly smile. "You sure 'bout that, brother?" I nod. "Then alright. How about a bet?"

"What bet?" I ask, already regretting saying anything.

"I bet that you can't go an entire week without havin' a drink."

Fucking Pyro. He's too fucking observant. I haven't been able to sleep without either fucking or drinking. He's putting me to the test. There's one thing he knows I can't do and that's turn a fucking bet down. "And if I do, what do I get in return?"

"Whatever the fuck you want, brother."

I nod. "If I go a week without touching a fucking drop of booze, then you and the rest of the brothers, along with your old ladies, stop this shit of askin' me if I'm okay. I'm as good as I'll ever be and there's nothin' that's goin' to change that outcome. Deal?"

He holds out his hand and I shake on it. "You've got yourself a deal. But you fucked up, brother—I was gonna get everyone to stop anyway."

Fuck!

"Now, you don't want to talk about the past. How about the girl? Ailbhe, right?"

Ah, the woman who's never far from my mind. Since we agreed to be fuck buddies, I've been able to sleep. The woman is so fucking insatiable that by the time I'm finished fucking her and make it home, I'm collapsing into bed and passing out until morning.

It's been a week, and there's not a night that goes by without us finding somewhere to have our hookups. We've been using a hotel, something I've been booking. I should probably find an apartment. It would be a fuck of a lot cheaper.

"What about Ailbhe?" I ask, wondering what he's getting at.

"Just wondering when you're goin' to be bringin' her around. The women want to meet her."

I laugh. He means his woman and sister. "Yeah, that ain't goin' to happen. I love Hayley and Chloe, but Christ, I know what they're like. That's not happenin'."

He chuckles. "Yeah, I don't blame you. Those two are desperate for more women around here."

"They like the club whores," I say with a grin. It isn't surprising, as the club whores also work at the club and know the deal.

Connor, the prospect, slides a beer toward me, but I shake my head, ignoring the way Pyro grins.

"Who's the bozo that's parked their bike against the fucking gate, meaning no one can get in?" I hear a deep voice say, and turn my head, shocked as fuck to see Danny Gallagher standing in the doorway of the clubhouse, both Wrath and Raptor standing beside him. "Gotta say, the club turned out a lot better than I expected. You've done a great job." His gaze moves to me. "Good to see you, Preacher. Man, it's been a while. I swear I did a double take when I saw you. I thought it was Jesus Christ himself sitting there."

I can't help but chuckle. My hair and beard have both gotten a little wild lately, and while I know they need tidying up, I ain't changing them just yet. Not when Ailbhe tugs on them when I'm fucking her hard.

"Oh shit," Connor says from behind me. "That's my bike. Sorry, Danny, I'll move it."

Danny grins. "You may want to check you've not damaged it."

Pyro and I glance at one another and then to Wrath and Raptor. All three brothers are wearing the same grin, and I have a feeling it matches mine.

"Okay, what have I missed?" Chloe asks. "It's kind of cool and creepy that you've all had a conversation without actually uttering a word."

"Connor just got his road name, babe," Py tells her.

Callie's lips part as her shoulders shake with laughter. "That's ironic, don't you think?"

"Yep," I reply as I lean back and cross my arms over my chest. Connor is a fucking genius. I mean, the guy could probably work for NASA or some shit like that, he's that fucking smart. "But the man's goin' to be made a club member in the next few weeks and he needs a road name."

It's funny, our road names are always given to us by others. Mine is very much like Connor's, the complete opposite of who I am. I was named Preacher because of who my parents were and the fact that me and my brother are called Kane and Abel. I despise anything to do with religion on the basis of how I grew up. I don't blame the church or any religious leader for what happened to me and my brother. That was down to my parents using what they believed the Bible taught them, and using it in a way to harm and belittle those they were supposed to protect. Religion isn't something I'd ever seek out. It's not something I want in my life or anywhere near me.

"Do we all have to call him Bozo?" Callie asks with a small smile. "Would it not be mean? Like, the guy's the smartest man in the room, and calling him a word that means stupid or significant seems a little..." she pauses as she tries to find the right word.

"Love that you think that, Mrs. Gallagher," Bozo says as he steps into the clubhouse wearing a smile.

"But being called Bozo isn't mean and isn't meant in that way."

Chloe nods as she reaches for her mom's hand. "It means that he's part of the family."

Yep, that's exactly it. He's a Fury Viper now. Just as the other three prospects are. Tyrone, Ciaran, and Oisin have all been given their road names already. Tyrone is Tank, as the man's built like one. Ciaran is Cowboy. The man got the name as someone said he was like one with all the dodgy dealings he'd been doing. And then there's Oisin, who's now called Hustler. The man can't do anything without trying to hustle someone. The only person who hadn't been given a road name was Connor, and now he's got it.

"But that doesn't mean I won't give Danny shit every time I see him for me having this road name."

I chuckle. That's something we've all done. While his road name isn't as great as others, his sticks out and he's going to fucking own it.

"Now that's sorted," Py says. "Not that we're not glad to see you, but is there a reason you're here, Danny?"

"You four got a minute?" he asks and Py nods. "Office?" Danny questions, and Pyro gets to his feet with Raptor and Wrath while I follow behind.

"What's this about?" Pyro asks once the office door is closed.

"You ever heard of Jed O'Connor?" he asks, and I glance around the room, wondering if I'm the only person who has no fucking idea who the hell that is. Thankfully, I'm not. Everyone has the same blank expression.

"Should we?" Pyro questions.

Danny takes a seat, making himself at home. "Jed O'Connor has always been a low life. He's a loan shark. He's always been on the lower side of the operations as the Kelly's had the top spot. As we all know, the Kelly's business took a huge fucking hit when both Sean's were taken out."

Yeah, those bastards shouldn't have targeted Chloe. Had they not, then maybe old man Kelly would still be alive. As for the younger Sean, no one knows what happened to him. The lore on the street is that someone mangled him up pretty good. From the sounds of it, they took a fucking chainsaw to him in bed and cut every limb from his body. No one has ever been arrested for it. It sounds like it was an inside job, but I have a feeling it was a fucking lot more than that. I've met Denis Gallagher. I know what he's like when his kids are targeted, and from what I've seen, he'll do whatever it takes to ensure his children are safe. Sean Jr was Chloe's biological father. If I were Denis, I would have done everything to make my daughter safe, and if

I were a betting man, I'd lay everything I have down on Denis being the man who took him out.

"So, what have the Kelly's got to do with this Jed guy?" Wrath asks.

"When the Kelly operation sank, Jed swooped in and started to pick up pace. Now, Jed is a bastard. From what I have heard, Jed's taking payment in other ways. So far, there have been three people who have told me they know someone this has happened to. Three different people."

"What are we talkin' about here, Danny?" Pyro asks, his voice vibrating with anger.

We have a feeling we know what Danny's saying, but before we lose our shit, we need confirmation.

"Jed O'Connor loans money and continues to loan money to people he knows won't be able to pay him back, and when he calls in for that payment, he will then take it in any way he can. Including taking their wives, children, and mothers."

"He's rapin' them?" Raptor hisses. "That's what you're tellin' us?"

Danny's jaw clenches. "That's what I've heard. Right now, Da's trying to find out if it's true."

If it is true then Jed is going to be in for a world of hurt. Not only do the Gallagher's not allow that shit to happen, but we don't either. That's never going to be done on our turf. Jed's going to be in for a rude awakening if he's doing that shit. He'll find out what happens when you fuck with the Vipers.

CHAPTER 9
AILBHE

I stare at the gorgeous man who's watching me with so much heat in his brown eyes, it makes my stomach flip. God, I adore the way he watches me. It's as though I'm the only person in the world. It makes me feel wanted and beautiful. I've never felt this way. Never felt so wanted.

He's half naked, which is a damn shame, but his top is off, which means I get a front row seat to that amazing chest of his. He doesn't have a six pack, but he doesn't need one. He's tall, big, and so damn sexy.

"You're overdressed there, babe," he says with a smirk. "You enjoyin' the view?"

I feel my cheeks heat. Damn him. Why the hell do I feel as though I'm a child being caught out?

I reach for the hem of my tee and pull it over my head. I'm not wearing a bra, and I grin as I hear his swift intake of breath. "We're even now," I tell him as my hands slide to the waistband of my leggings.

"You like gettin' dirty, babe?" he growls, that sound making goosebumps pop up along my skin.

"With you," I say, staring him in the eye. "Absolutely."

I can't deny it. Being with Preacher is something I love to do. Things between us are easy. It's great to have something—someone—I'm able to be carefree around and just be myself. I don't have to worry about homework, dinner, or checking that everyone is doing okay. I'm able to be me, not a mam.

He slowly undoes the fly of his jeans, and the sound of the zipper is the only sound that can be heard in the room. He wants me just as much as I want him. I smirk as he kicks off his pants, and I move to the bed, knowing things are about to heat up. This man can make me go from zero to a hundred with just a heated look. He knows how to get me worked up, and the best thing about it is I do the exact same for him.

I'm nowhere near experienced. Hell, Preacher is all I know, and God, it was an amazing experience to start out with. I'm not looking too far into it. I'm just enjoying being with him. He's showing me what he likes and I'm finding out what I like too.

I lie on the bed, my knees bent with my feet on the

sheets. I spread my legs and give him a glimpse of my pussy.

"Teasin' me, babe?" he growls. It's a sound that I fucking love.

"Don't know what you're talking about," I reply, my voice breathy.

He shakes his head. His thick, long hair is up in a bun, and I know that by the time we're finished, it's going to be down. I love pulling on it while we're having sex. He stalks toward me, his cock thick and standing to attention. He's huge. Fuck, I'm still not used to how big he is, but he's more aware of it now, rather than the brutal way he took me the first time. I think he believes he hurt me, and while it did hurt in the beginning, the pain ebbed away, and then I loved everything he did to me.

He climbs onto the bed, positioning himself between my legs, his cock thick against my wet pussy. My hands slide around his neck and our mouths fuse together. I love how he kisses me. There's nothing better than the way he dominates me when we're together. My hands move up to his hair as his move to my hips. I pull the tie from his hair just as he tilts my hips. I gasp as he plunges his cock into me. He's so fucking big, I feel full of him.

"Preacher," I whimper, loving the way he stretches me. "More," I moan, needing to feel him deeper.

He withdraws slightly and then pushes his cock into me, feeding it inch by inch. There's a little pain from him stretching me, but the pleasure by far outweighs that. Once again, he's taking care of me, making sure that I'm not hurting, giving me the time to adjust to him.

"Fuck, Ailbhe," he growls, thrusting deep inside of me. "You're so fuckin' tight."

"God," I groan, my fingers tangling in his hair, my body moving beneath his. I'm matching him thrust for thrust. I can't get enough of him.

He rotates his hips, thrusting harder and harder into me.

"Harder," I plead, needing more.

"Fuckin' perfect," he hisses, his fingers tightening on my hips, biting into the flesh. I grind down on his cock as he thrusts into me. "That's it, babe, so fuckin' good."

His praise makes me preen. I fucking love that he's praising me.

"Preacher," I whisper, unsure how to communicate that I need more. A lot fucking more.

He raises his head and looks at me. His thrusts become brutal, each one deliberate and precise. Hitting deep inside me. His intense gaze makes me shiver as I grind against him.

He releases his hands from my hips without

missing a beat as he continues to thrust hard and deep. His hands slide up my body, leaving goosebumps in their wake. My body is burning with need.

"I've got you," he says thickly. "Trust me?"

I nod, unsure of what he's going to do, but I do trust him with me sexually.

His hand slides around my neck, almost as though he's cuffing me. "You want me to stop, you tug on my hair," he growls.

"Okay," I say, feeling as though I need to answer him verbally rather than just a nod.

He flashes me that sexy grin of his, and I know I did the right thing. His other hand moves to my neck; not hard, but he has a decent grip.

"If you want to stop, what do you do?" he says thickly. Those brown eyes of his are filled with so much heat and intensity, I swallow hard.

Heat pools between my legs. "Tug on your hair," I reply, my voice a little breathy.

His hands tighten a little more and I gasp, surprised but not panicked. I'm rather intrigued by what's about to happen. He stops fucking me and instead focuses on what he's doing with his hands.

He tightens a little more, keeping away from the front of my throat and focusing on the sides. I feel my breath start to leave me, and my body heats with want. God, it feels so fucking good.

Once again he tightens his hand, and then he starts to fuck me again, his thrusts just as brutal as they were before. My lips part, a moan lodged in my throat as his hands keep their grip on me.

I feel my pleasure start to rise. My entire body feels as though it's burning. I'm ready to erupt. But Preacher releases my neck, and I pull in a deep breath as he thrusts into me deeply before staying there.

"You like that, babe?" he questions, and I know damn well he knows what he's doing.

"Yes," I say a little roughly. "I was so close," I whine, hating that he brought me out of the zone.

He grins. "You goin' to come for me?" he growls.

"Yes, so fuck me," I hiss. My body is wound up so tightly, I'm ready to explode at the merest of touches.

He starts to fuck me again, not taking long to pick up his pace, until he's fucking me harder and faster than ever before. I guess I'm not the only one who's close to the edge.

"Yes," I hiss, his cock hitting me deep and in just the right spot.

His hands go back to my throat, and I smile. God yes. I want to feel that high of losing my breath, of being completely reliant on him. I want to feel that thrill.

"Fuck," he snarls as he grits his teeth, rotates his hips, and powers into me. "Fuck, it's goin' to be quick."

His hands tighten around my neck as he continues to pound into me.

My breath leaves me just as my pleasure spikes through me. God, I can feel it coming. My entire body is about to explode.

"Fuckin' come," he growls. "You need to come right fuckin' now," he snaps.

I gasp as his thrusts get harder and faster. My pleasure is skyrocketing, taking my breath away from me.

My orgasm hits me like a tornado ripping through me and sweeping me up in its path. He releases my neck and I gasp for air, and the feeling of the high intensifies my orgasm. "Preach," I gasp.

"So fuckin' perfect," he grunts as he pistons his cock in and out of me. His lips slam down against mine as he kisses me, his tongue sweeping into my mouth, consuming me even more. His thrusts are brutal but feel oh so fucking good, prolonging my orgasm.

I love when he gets like this. It means he's not holding back from me. Every bit of his control is gone. I love knowing I can do that to him.

"Fuck," he snarls. His cock swells and he thrusts deep into me. My pussy contracts around his cock, and he groans low and long. "Fuck, yeah, that's it, babe. Squeeze my cock. Good girl," he grunts as he spurts his cum inside of me. I preen at the praise once again. God, this man sure knows more about my sexual appetite and what I like than I do. I'm not sure how he knew what I wanted, especially when I didn't, but fuck, I'm glad he did.

"We'll definitely be doing that again," I say, my words husky as I try to regain my breath.

"Babe, have no fuckin' doubt. There's nothin' better in this world than watchin' you come. You light up brighter than anythin' I've ever seen."

Damn. He's so damn sweet when he wants to be.

He pulls out of me and I wince at the pain. It's only fleeting and it's well worth it. I quickly realize that once again, he didn't use a condom. It's happened twice now, and it's a reminder that I need to make an appointment with the doctor and get put on birth control. Preacher loses his mind and forgets about a condom.

"Shower," I say with a smile as I slide off the bed and reach for my clothes.

This is the worst part about having this sort of relationship with Preacher. It's just sex, so once we're done and I shower, it's time for me to leave. I don't usually get home now until around four-ish, and then I have to be up by seven to get the kids up and ready for school. I'm napping a hell of a lot more during the day now. I'm still in beauty school, trying to get everything together. It'll take me a while to graduate, but I'm doing okay and I'm loving life right now.

I take a long, hot shower, a little bummed when Preacher doesn't join me—something he usually does. But I'm glad to be clean. I glance at my phone and see it's almost three-thirty. It's time for me to get going and go home. I'm not working tomorrow, which means I can have an early night and catch up on the lack of sleep.

"Here," Preacher says as I exit the bathroom. I'm fully dressed and ready to leave.

I'm shocked when I look at him. He's holding a pizza box. I frown.

"You got us pizza?" I ask, confused. This is new, something we've never done.

He shrugs. "We worked up an appetite, and you need to eat."

I smile at him. It's the sweetest thing anyone's ever done for me. "Thank you."

He places the box on the tiny table he has in the room and reaches for a slice. "Hope you like meat."

I smirk as I glance at his crotch. "Definitely."

He chuckles. "You're fuckin' crazy, you know that, babe?"

I take a slice of pizza and sit on the chair. "Honestly, I'm not. It's a side of me only you bring out."

He watches me carefully. Those deep brown eyes are assessing me. "Truth be told, I ain't much fun these days. But havin' fun with you is definitely on the top of my priority list."

I raise a brow. "You have a list? Okay, stud, let's hear it."

"Fuckin' you, ridin' my bike, and bein' with my brothers."

I nod. "That's a thorough list," I quip as I take a bite of pizza. I can't help the moan that escapes my lips as I do. It tastes so damn good.

"Keep that up, babe, and I'll be bendin' you over the bed and fuckin' you until you pass out."

My cheeks flush at his words. Damn him. "You're the crazy one. So, this bike of yours... did you have it imported from America?"

He grins. "I did. How did you know? It cost a fuckin' fortune. Thankfully, Raptor was able to sort it for me. He was movin' over and he had more time than I did. It took a while but he managed to have it here when he arrived."

"How long have you had it? I mean, I don't know much about bikes. Do they last as long as cars? I've got a 2007 Yaris. It's small but reliable."

"It depends what vehicles you're comparin', babe, but bikes are good. They'll last most people a lifetime."

"What made you want to join the Fury Vipers? I mean, we have the Devil Falcons MC here along with the Fury Vipers now, but I don't really know them. Are there a lot of motorcycle clubs in America?"

He grins at me, and it makes my heart race. "There's enough," he tells me. "I randomly bumped into a guy one day who invited him to a Fury Viper party. The guy turned out to be a douche, but the moment I met the Viper guys, I found my home. You ever get that feeling?"

I pause for a second. Did he not feel that with his family? I want to ask so many questions, but I'm trying really hard not to push too far. I'm keeping to relatively neutral questions in hope of getting to know him better, but trying to keep all the private things out. "I have a big family. There're six of us kids. It's taken a while, but over the past couple of months, I've actually felt like I belong."

He nods. "So you plan on bein' a stripper for a while?"

Okay, that wasn't the question I expected him to ask. "I don't know. Right now, it's paying for school and rent. I'll keep doing it until I don't need to any longer. It's great money and I seem to be good at it."

He raises a brow at me. "Seem to be?" he scoffs. "Babe, watchin' you dance gives me a fucking hard on. You ooze sexiness without even tryin'. Trust me, you're fuckin' good at it."

Compliments aren't something I'm used to, so

hearing him give one to me so easily makes me blush. "Thanks."

We continue to talk about general things, not getting too deep into our lives. It's fun, and I feel as though it's not just fucking right now. Once the pizza is finished, I get to my feet. I really need to get home.

"You're off tomorrow, right?" he asks as he too rises to his feet.

I nod. "I am. I have to take my sisters to school though, so I'll be up bright and early."

"The hotel's paid for 'til twelve."

My heart stutters. He wants a daytime rendezvous? Hell yes. "I can be here for ten."

His lips twitch. "Then, babe, it's a fuckin' date."

I move toward the door. "See you then, Preacher."

"Drive safe, babe," he says thickly, and my heart soars.

Damn it, I'm going to get attached if he continues to be so sweet. I leave the hotel with a smile on my face. That was probably the greatest night of my life, and I'm lucky that I get to meet with him again tomorrow. I just pray that when what we have comes to an end, he doesn't treat me the way he did after our first night together. There are feelings involved now, and I don't know if I could deal with the shame and disappointment if he did it again.

CHAPTER 10
AILBHE

My stomach flips as I run to the bathroom, unable to keep the vomit at bay any longer. Fuck. Over and over again, I vomit, until there's nothing left in my stomach. I sit back against the wall, my feet pressed against the cold, tiled floor, and rest my head on my knees. Four days in a row now this has been happening. I can't deny it any longer. Nausea, tender breasts, and a missed period—they all point to one thing. On shaky legs, I stand and reach for the brown paper bag containing the stupid box that I purchased at the pharmacy yesterday. I hid it, praying I wouldn't have to use it, but I can't pretend for another day.

I read through the instructions, trying my hardest not to cry. I have no idea what to even think right now.

I take the test, and while I wait the three minutes

required for the result, I close my eyes and pray that it's negative. I don't have the capability to look after another child. We're barely surviving as it is. Da's making things even worse by continuing to be an arsehole who just comes and goes as he pleases, and Ruairi's talking about moving out and finding his own place. I have no idea how I'll manage with another child, let alone a baby. I can't be pregnant. There's just no way I can be. I need this test to be negative.

I take a steadying breath, swallow the tears clogged in my throat, and open my eyes. The tears I managed to keep at bay begin to fall. I knew it. There was no other explanation for my symptoms other than pregnancy, and now it's confirmed. God, what am I going to do?

For almost two months now, Preacher and I have been having sex, and it's good, great even. But he was very clear about the terms of our relationship right from the start. It's only sex, nothing more. I agreed, my life is chaotic enough, there's no way I could cope with anything else on my plate. Now I'm adding a baby into the mix. God, this isn't good, I don't even know how I'm going to be able to manage it all. Damn it, I can't even think straight.

I sink to the bathroom floor and cry. I never intended for this to happen. God, my life has changed so much over the past year. Every dream I had has gone down the pan. I'm barely able to catch my breath with everything changing so much. And now a baby? Ugh, what the hell am I going to do?

I end my pity party when I hear someone start to move around in their bedroom. I need to get dressed and start the day. The children will be up and about soon, and I don't need them to worry about anything. I don't want to tell anyone yet as I have no idea what I'm going to do. The first thing I need to do is call the doctor and confirm that I am indeed pregnant, and then I can start to make decisions.

I bin the pregnancy test, unable to even look at it right now. I take a deep breath and sigh as I look in the mirror. I look as though I've been sobbing. The puffy, red, watery eyes are a huge giveaway. I quickly scrub my face, cleaning it of tears, snot, and vomit. I don't want the children to worry. They've had such upheavals in their lives already; the last thing I want for them is to wonder what's going to happen when they've finally started to have a stable life.

Once I'm finished in the bathroom, I quickly make my way to my bedroom, managing to make it there without bumping into anyone, which is a hard feat considering there are four other people in the house. I need space away from everyone, I need to be able to process this properly. I need to figure out how the hell I'm going to tell Preacher.

"Morning," Ruairi says as he enters the kitchen three hours later. All the kids have been fed and are in the sitting room watching TV while I clean. Evie's lying on the sofa, thumb in mouth as she watches. She usually gets like that when she's coming down with something. I pray that she doesn't, and that if she does, whatever it is, it passes quickly.

"Morning," I reply. "Hungry?" I ask, biting back the urge to close my eyes. Since I woke up this morning, the pounding in my head has slowly gotten worse. I'm no stranger to headaches, but the ones that cause pain in your eyes are the worst.

He shakes his head. "No, I'm fine, thanks, Al. I've got four apartments to look at today. I'm going to take the kids with me. I'd like to have their approval too."

I give him a smile, my heart dropping at his words. God, that's the last thing I expected, and it couldn't come at a worse time. "You know there's no need for you to move out, right?"

He nods. "It's been hard living with you all again. I got used to my own space."

I laugh, and the sound feels forced even to my own ears. But I understand his need to move out. It's a big adjustment being back here and I know it's not been easy on him. "Well, I'm glad that you're here."

His eyes narrow as he watches me. "You okay?"

I plaster on a smile. "Yeah, of course. What time are you viewing the apartments?"

He glances at his watch. "In about an hour, so we'd best be going. Rest up today, Al. You look like shit."

I blink. Well, that's rude.

Before I can say anything, he continues, "Not to mention you were throwing up this morning. You're probably worn out. You need to rest and sleep."

Hell, sleep sounds like a good idea, but I don't know if I'll be able to fall back to sleep, not with my mind running wild like it is.

"Kids," Ruairi shouts, and I wince at how loud he is. "Get your coats on. We're going out."

As usual, the kids come running into the kitchen, glancing between both Ruairi and I.

"Where are we going?" Fiona asks. "And why isn't Ailbhe coming?"

I glance down at my pajamas and smile. Everyone is dressed and ready for the day except me.

"Ailbhe's sick," Evie says as she shuffles over to me. "I'm staying with Ailbhe. I'm sick too."

I press my hand against her forehead and feel that she's burning up. "You not feeling well, honey?"

She shakes her head. "I'm tired."

I reach down and pull her into my arms. She doesn't hesitate to wrap her arms around my neck and snuggle against me. I'll give her some medicine to bring down her temperature. Maybe going back to sleep is what'll be best for the both of us.

"You good with her?" Ruairi asks, and I roll my eyes. Of course I'm good with her. Who the hell does he think has been taking care of her?

I nod. "Yep. The kids don't need to go. I'll be here."

"You need rest," Mikey says, giving me a pointed look. "You've been taking care of us and now you're sick."

Hannah nods while Fiona moves toward the cupboard that houses all the medicine.

"Take these," she says, placing some tablets on the counter. "We can all tell that you have a headache, so don't deny it. Take those, give Evie some medicine, and then both of you go to bed," she instructs.

My lips twist as I try not to laugh at how stern she is. "Yes, mam. Anything else?"

She places her hands on her hips, eyebrow raised as she looks at me. "Less of the sass, thank you."

I can't hold my laughter back any longer. She's bloody hilarious. "Yes, mam. Now be good for Ruairi, okay?"

She nods. "Will do—as long as he's buying us lunch."

"Does this mean we're moving?" Hannah asks.

"No," I say softly, realizing she's worried. "Ruairi's

moving out as he's smelly and I can't take it any longer."

Hannah's shoulders droop as the tension leaves them. "Okay," she replies with a grin.

"Let's go," Ruairi tells them. "Both of you go to bed," he says, pointing at Evie and I.

"Can I sleep in your bed, Ailbhe?" Evie asks once we're upstairs. I've given her the medicine, which I know she wouldn't have asked for unless she was sick.

"Come on, sweetie," I say as I hold her hand and lead her into my room. I help her into the bed and climb in beside her.

"Night, Ailbhe," she whispers as she snuggles against me.

"Night, Evie. Hope you feel better soon."

It doesn't take her long to fall asleep. I close my eyes, listening to her soft snores, my mind whirling about the pregnancy. What the hell am I going to do?

First step: Get confirmation.

Second step: Don't freak out.

No matter what, it's going to be okay. There's no other choice, so it has to be.

CHAPTER 11
PREACHER

It's been a week since I last saw Ailbhe. I haven't been at the strip club due to there being a lot of club business that's needed to be taken care of. Tonight is also a no-go on seeing Ailbhe as my brothers and I are going to meet with Denis Gallagher and his son, Danny, to find out what the fuck is going on with Jed O'Connor. Everything has come back squeaky clean on the guy. A little too squeaky clean, in my opinion. No one is that fucking good.

My cell buzzes and I glance at the screen. Reaper. I grit my teeth as I slide my cell into my pocket. It's been over nine months since I last saw Reaper and Tyson, but it hasn't stopped Reaper from calling. I can't bring myself to answer the call and talk to him. I know he's feeling guilty for having Tyson, when he shouldn't be. But watching someone else raise my boy isn't something I can do right now, hence why I moved across the world to get away. I know that it's fucked up. Reaper's my brother, the closest thing I have to actual family, and he's my best friend. He deserves better than to be ignored, but I just can't listen to him talk about Tyson.

"He's been askin' about you," Wrath says as he stands beside me.

We're currently out at the docks. It's fucking cold, but it's secluded. The only people around are us as we wait for the Gallaghers. Denis has the right people in his pockets. The security firm that's supposed to be watching this end of the docks is currently having issues with an incident happening about a ten-minute drive from here. They'll be busy for the next hour or so, giving us enough time to ensure that whatever business we have is done.

"Has he?" I say, knowing damn well that he has been. Every fucking day the brothers are catching up with one or all of the brothers from New York. It's been a huge fucking change; not just the food, but the culture, and the people, not to mention the weather. It's always raining. It never fucking ends. I'm surprised by how much I actually enjoy being here. I thought it would be a pit stop for me, but I'm contemplating making it permanent.

"You're a fuckin', asshole, brother, you know that?"

I grin at him. "Look, I get that he's worried, but for my own sanity, this is the way it's gotta be."

"I get that," he says quietly. "I don't know how the fuck you're still standing, brother. I really don't. Leaving Eva for weeks was hard. It almost broke me. I can't imagine losing her or James."

"I pray that you never have to," I reply, my chest aching from the heaviness that's been settled on it for months. I would never wish this pain on my worst enemy.

"But you've got to talk to Reap, man. He's worried about you. He's the closest thing you have to family. You need to talk to him."

I grit my teeth. "Right now, Wrath, I need to focus on myself and makin' it through each day."

The struggle to wake up every morning is real. I lie in bed and wonder why the fuck I should even rise. Sleep is my only solitude, it's the only time I'm able to escape the pain and it takes a fucking lot to make me pass out to a point I don't think about Tyson or Abel. A bottle of whiskey would usually do it, if I were to drink that, I wouldn't have to worry about the night. I'd be passed out. But I know doing that isn't going to help. It won't help me and it won't help my brothers. So I force myself to get out of bed every morning, and try to make it through the night without dreaming then, I push myself to get dressed and go about my day. It's fucking hard, but I have to do it.

"What do you need, Preach? What can we do to help?"

I shake my head. "Nothin'," I say honestly. "There's nothin' you can do, brother. This is somethin' I'm goin' to have to figure out for myself."

I hear his heavy sigh. I get it; if the tables were turned, I'd feel the exact same way. I'd want to help my brother; take him out of that dark place mentally; help him find a way through it. But I can't let anyone in. There's nothing anyone can say to me to make this better. It's a fucked up situation all around and I'm trying my fucking hardest to make it through each day. Not drinking isn't fucking helping either. Goddamn Pyro. I was so fucking stupid to take that bet. Especially now that I haven't seen Ailbhe in a damn week. Fucking her helps me sleep without the alcohol.

The sound of a car engine grows closer and we stand taller. A sleek Mercedes pulls into the dock, and right behind it is a dark Range Rover. Denis, Danny, and Malcolm Gallagher step out of the Mercedes and two men jump out of the Range Rover.

"Pyro, Raptor, Wrath, and Preacher," Denis says as he joins us. "You all know my sons, Danny and Malcolm." He nods to his boys. "This is Stephen Maguire and Maverick O'Hara. Callie's brothers."

Ah, I've heard about Stephen and Maverick. They helped Makenna's cousin's in-laws out when they were in a tight spot a little while ago. Stephen has a reputation within the criminal world, not only here in Ireland but around the world. It wasn't until recently that people found out it was Stephen who has the moniker, the Eraser. The man has a special way of getting rid of his enemies, and while I have yet to see it in practice, I've heard that it's twisted and sickening to those who have watched it. No one wants to elaborate on the ways that he kills, but it's going to be fun to find out what it is exactly. As for Maverick, he goes by the moniker, the Cleaner. That's because he has a penchant for using chemicals to get rid of his enemies. The man's smart as a tack and is damn well genius enough to understand chemical formulas that can get rid of bodies.

"It's nice to meet you," Maverick says as he holds out his hand for us to shake. Pyro goes first and the rest follow. "Callie and Chloe have all good things to say about you. Of course, we've heard about your reputation. I hope the rumors are half as good as the real thing."

I chuckle. "That they are," I tell him with a grin. "The same could be said for the two of you."

"Oh, you have no idea how good they are," Stephen replies.

"Now," Denis says, glancing at Stephen and shaking his head. "We're here because this is a place that is secure and we can't be overheard."

"As is the clubhouse," Pyro says through gritted teeth.

"It is," Stephen says with a nod. "But we're all being watched. We're always being fucking watched. The guardai aren't ever going to stop watching us. They'll never have anything on us, but they've got our homes on lockdown with surveillance."

"Here I thought you had the cops in your pocket, Denis," Pyro taunts.

"Not all of them, but enough to ensure we're never followed. Now, we need to talk about Jed."

"That cunt is going down," Stephen hisses. "Not going to lie, Denis, I'm going to get sick and tired of waiting for some actual proof the guy's a fucking prick. I'll end him, no bother at all."

Maverick nods. "Might as well. It's not like the fucker's actually doing anything for us. From what Gerry's said, he's encroaching into all our territories."

"You can't just kill people for the sake of it," Denis sighs.

"Says the man who has done so on more than one occasion," Maverick snorts. "What's so different about this fucker?"

"He's being watched," Danny tells us. "He's on the

guardai radar, as are we. That bastard dies and we'll be the number one suspects. None of us want to do time for that fucker."

He's got a point, but I'm still for the idea of taking Jed out. Everyone knows there's no smoke without fire. Those rumors aren't fake. Jed's up to something and we're going to find out what the fuck it is. That asshole's business is going to end and he won't be taking payment from anyone else.

"Tonight, word is that Jed has a meeting with someone who owes him thirty grand," Malcolm informs us.

Pyro lets out a whistle. "Damn, that's a lot of money to owe someone. How the fuck has he racked up that much debt?"

"It gets worse," Malcolm says. "He's not the one paying it off. From what I've uncovered, it's his kids paying it off."

My stomach rolls with acid. What man does that shit? That's beyond fucked up. Christ, what an ass.

"The meeting should be taking place in about an hour. It's happening not far from here," Danny says as he glances at his cell. "We should get going."

I hate this shit. We have little to no information on what's going to happen. We're going in blind. I trust my brothers implicitly, but there are other factors involved here, so I have to go with those who have helped us.

My brothers and I climb onto our bikes while the rest of the men get into their cars. We follow behind them as they lead us to where Jed O'Connor is to have his meeting with this fucked up mystery guy.

It takes us almost thirty minutes to get to the meeting point. It's in a parking lot, across from a narrow, one-way street, we've the perfect vantage point to see the bar, one that I've seen many times but haven't frequented. It's rowdy and looks like a fucking mess. There are drunken assholes stumbling around the place, and it just looks sketchy as hell.

"Ah, the man of the hour," Denis comments as I see a tall guy in his mid-fifties step out of the bar. He's got three men around him, all of whom are taller than him and have about a hundred pounds more muscle than he does. It's clear to see that he's a lot more than just a loan shark. No one would have that much muscle behind them just being a loan shark.

"Peter Mangan," Jed says loudly, and the drunken asshole who's walking toward the bar stumbles a little as he raises his head. "Been looking for you."

"J-J-Jed, I didn't know you were in town," the guy shouts.

I roll my eyes. Christ, he's drunk as fuck.

"Evidently," Jed says. "Where's my money?"

The guy's face pales. "I told you, Al is getting you the money. Talk to her."

"I would," Jed grunts. "But I haven't seen her either. You and your family seem to be hiding from me."

"She's home," the asshole Peter says, his voice cracking. He's scared and everyone knows it.

Jed stands taller. "She had better have my money, Peter. If she doesn't, I'm not going to let her get away with it."

The asshole holds up his hands. "I know the rules, Jed, and so does she."

"I'll be seeing you real soon, Peter. You'd best pray that your daughter has the money. She's real pretty, and I have no doubt she'd be a fucking animal if I got between her thighs She doesn't pay up, I'm taking payment anyway," he snarls as he turns on his heel and returns to the bar.

"So, we were right," Denis grunts. "That cunt. I'm going to enjoy killing the fucker."

"We need to find out who the fuck that guy Peter is and who his daughter is. God, fucking Jed, the slimy bastard," Maverick hisses. "I'll have Freddie ask around. He's able to get information from everyone."

Danny chuckles. "As long as he's not on the rob, we should be good."

"Freddie Kinnock, also known as the Thief of Dublin," Malcolm tells us, and I grin. Now him I have heard of. The guy is a well known thief, from stealing wallets to cracking safes. He's a handy guy to have on your team.

"Yep," Maverick says. "He'll find out everything we need to know. I'm just hoping he'll have the information tonight."

If he doesn't, then fuck, some woman's going to be hurt because of Jed's fucking bullshit.

CHAPTER 12
AILBHE

There's a loud knock on the door. I grimace as I get to my feet. I've just gotten the kids off to school and was hoping to go back to sleep for a bit. This morning sickness is kicking my arse and I don't see it stopping any time soon. I have an appointment with the doctor tomorrow for confirmation.

There's another knock. This time it's louder and the pounding causes the doorframe to shake. Whoever the fuck is there, they're in a hurry to see me.

I open the door, and I'm shocked to see Jed O'Connor standing on my doorstep. He's accompanied by two of his bodyguards, and all three of them are eyeing me with anger and caution. This is the last thing I bloody need first thing in the morning. "Is there something I can help you with?"

Jed doesn't answer me right away. Instead, he pushes past me and into the house.

"Hey," I call out, unable to hide my shock and irritation. "You can't just barge into my house. What the hell is your problem?"

"Girl," Jed says, his words filled with contempt, "you'd best remember who you're talking to."

I cross my arms over my chest and stare at him. I haven't moved from the door and I have no intention of doing so. "What's going on? Why are you here?"

"You owe me money, Ailbhe. A lot of money. We had a deal," he tells me.

"Yes, we do have a deal. Every Monday morning, at least a thousand euro is to be put into your account."

His jaw clenches as he glares at me. "That's correct, but you're a week late."

I jolt back at his words. "The hell I am," I hiss. "Every Monday I meet with your stupid goon and pay the money. Last week, not only did I pay it, but I gave two thousand euro and he marked it off for me on my book, just as he does every week."

I have a book that tallies how much I owe Jed and how much I'm paying off. The arsehole Tony marks it off each week as I pay him. I also meet him in a busy location where I know there are security cameras, so if shit like this happens, I'll always have proof.

"Show me," Jed snaps.

I roll my eyes. "I don't have the book right now. My brother's currently meeting with him to pay this week's money."

Jed glances at his watch. "What time is he coming back?"

I frown. "How the hell am I supposed to know? I'm not his keeper. You need to talk with Tony. This is bullshit. I met him outside the post office on O'Connell Street. With the money and connections you have, you'll be able to check that yourself."

Jed closes the distance between us. The smell of cigarettes and whiskey on his breath is awful and makes me want to heave.

"If I find out you're lying, Ailbhe, you had better hide," he snarls, pushing closer into my space. "You owe me a fucking lot of money, and I'm going to be paid one way or another."

I press my arms around me tighter. "What's that supposed to mean?" I ask, trying my hardest not to sound as though I'm intimidated. Everyone's heard the rumors of what Jed does to those who don't pay up. Not to mention what Da said to me about what he's promised Jed—me, any way Jed wants. I have no doubt that Jed will do exactly that. Whatever the hell he wants.

"You'd just better be praying you're telling the truth," he snaps.

"Why would I lie? Have I not paid on time before?"

He works his jaw, his gaze roaming along my body. "There's always a first time for everything."

Christ, he truly is a sleazy bastard.

"Well, not this time. I paid Tony the money last week and Ruairi's paying Tony money today."

"That's a real shame," he says thickly. "I've been waiting to take my turn with you. I can't wait to get between those thighs of yours. I heard that you've got a sexy body beneath all those baggy clothes."

Ugh, God, he really is an arsehole. There's no way in hell that I'd ever let him anywhere near me. Fuck no. He'd have to kill me first. "Don't worry, Jed, I'll continue to pay the money on time."

Even his smile makes me want to shiver in disgust. "I wouldn't be opposed if you didn't."

"Why? That makes no sense. Surely you'd rather have the money."

He runs his finger along my cheek, and it takes everything that I have inside of me not to recoil. "Money? I have loads of that. But taking women like you, so perfect, beautiful, and defiant... I can see it in your eyes—the sound of your screams as I take you would be worth more than money could buy."

"So basically, you love raping women and you get away with it as you call it payment?"

"You don't have to be so crass about it. It's not at all as bad as you make it out to be."

I blink. "If you say so. But you can count me out. There's not a hope in hell you'll ever get me on my back. I'll keep paying the debt."

His fingers linger a little too long on my skin before he takes a step backward. "Shame. But you shouldn't ever say never."

God, he's so fucking repulsive. "I do have a question," I say. "Why would you make me pay a debt that doesn't belong to me?"

"Kin is kin, sweetheart. Your father needs his debt paid and you started to pay it. What else was I supposed to do, kill your father?"

I lift my shoulders and shrug. "If it meant him paying, then yes, you should have."

He steps back and tuts. "Now, Ailbhe, that's not a nice thing to say about your father."

I stare at him. "That man practically sold me and his other kids to you. I have no love for a man like that. Hell, I have no love for a man who has no morals."

"You mean me?" he questions, his eyebrows practically hitting his hairline. "I have morals. Just because they don't align with yours, it doesn't mean I don't have them."

"What the fuck is going on here?" I hear Ruairi roar. I turn to see him running down the street toward the house. "Get the fuck away from her," he snarls as he pushes into the house and positions himself in front of me.

"Ah, Ruairi, lovely to see you, as always. Now, could you show me the payment book?"

Ruairi looks to me and his brows furrow. "What's going on?"

"Tony didn't give Jed the money we paid last week, so Jed here is out two grand and is looking for payment." I can't keep the disdain out of my voice. I dislike Jed more than I have ever disliked anyone in my life, and that's saying a lot seeing as both of my parents are bastards.

Ruairi reaches into his pocket and pulls out the book. "Whatever the fuck Tony's deal is, Jed, it's Tony's deal, not ours. You don't come around here, again. You hear me?"

Jed doesn't look at Ruairi. Instead, he flips through the book. I notice his eyes narrow and darken when he reaches the page for this week and last week.

"Very well," he says as he hands Ruairi the book back. "Remember what I said, Ailbhe. If you don't make the payment, I'll take it another way."

My stomach rolls at the thought of him touching me. There's no way in hell that will ever happen.

"The payments will be made," Ruairi assures him.

"Now, I think it's past time you all left. You've had your payment for today. Go."

I breathe a sigh of relief when they do as he says and leave my home. I'm able to breathe a little easier, but I'm not able to stop shaking. God, I'm glad Ruairi returned home when he did. I'd hate to think what would have happened had he not.

"He ever calls to this house again, Al, you do not fucking open that door," Ruairi says, his eyes wild. "That cunt is up to no good."

I hold my hands up. "Trust me, I know. The man's a sleazebag. There's no way in hell I'm opening that door to him again."

"Thank fuck for that. The last thing you need is for me to be doing time. He comes here again, I'll kill him."

For the first time in my life, I actually believe he could do it. He's made plenty of threats in the past, but this time, I really think he means it.

God help Jed if he does come round again.

CHAPTER 13
AILBHE

ONE MONTH LATER

Today's the day. I can't hide it anymore. I need to talk with Preacher. I've had the pregnancy confirmed. The test was correct—I'm pregnant. I'm actually six weeks along, which is really early. I'm still terrified, but after talking it through with Ruairi who realized a few days after I found out, I realized that it would be okay. That I've managed to find a way to be a mam to our younger siblings, and having a baby in the mix will be hard, but I can do it.

I was a little confused as to how he knew, but I soon realized that he's not stupid and with me being sick every morning it wasn't hard to figure it out.

Once the kids had gone to school, he sat me down and we spoke. There were so many tears, it was cathartic. Ruairi let me know that no matter what, I wasn't alone and he would be here to help. He has asked about the father, but I haven't told him who it is. I think I'm more scared of telling Preacher about the baby than anything. I have no idea how he's going to react, and that's what has me scared the most.

"Ailbhe," I hear Hannah yell. There's fear in her voice.

My feet move quickly as I rush toward her. "What's going on?" I ask as I reach the front door and see that she's opened it.

"Ailbhe?" I hear the low tone and look up, shocked to see Freddie Kinnock standing at my door. "It's been a while. You doing okay?"

"Hey, Freddie," I say with a smile as I step in front of Hannah. "Honey, why don't you go play in your room? I'm going to talk with Freddie. He's a friend of Ruairi's."

Hannah nods and flashes me a smile. "Bye," she says and runs up the stairs.

I turn back to Freddie. "Come in, but Ruairi's not here."

He steps into the house. "I'm not here to see Ruairi, Ailbhe. I'm here to see you."

Now that's shocking. "Um, okay. What's going on?"

We take a seat on the sofa and I wait for him to get to the point of why he's here.

"Your da's a piece of shit, Ailbhe," he tells me.

I can't help but laugh. "Yeah, tell me something I don't know. Christ, Freddie, Da's been a prick for years. You only just realizing that?"

His lips twitch. "Knew it for a long while, but I found out about a month ago just how fucked up he is. I never realized it was your da, though, Ailbhe. I hadn't seen him in years."

My brows furrow. "What happened?"

He sighs. "It's shit that I have to be the one to tell you this. Your da owes Jed O'Connor thirty grand."

Ah, so that's what this is about. "Yeah, it was over forty and now it's down to twenty-six."

His eyes widen at my words. "You took four grand off in four weeks?"

"How did you know I was the one paying it off?" I'm not surprised that he knows everything. Then again, I'm shocked Da's let it be known that he's a fucking dick and making his child pay for everything.

"Jed had a very loud conversation outside the Shebeen pub last month, where he let it be known that he was tired of waiting for money from your da. However, your da was a dick and told him 'Al' was paying it. Didn't realize it was you he was talking about. But it was fucked up, and I've been looking into it since then. I found out last week that it was you. Imagine my surprise when I also found out you're still living at home. What the fuck happened?"

"Nosey fucker, aren't you, Freddie?" I ask. "How's Ava? I haven't seen her in a while."

The easygoing smile leaves his face. "She's grand. Same old Ava. You know that."

"Not nice when someone dives into your life, is it?"

He releases a heavy sigh. "Christ, Ailbhe, I'm trying to be nice and help you."

"I appreciate that, and it was a low blow asking about Ava. I'm sorry." Everyone knows Ava is off-limits. They have a very tumultuous relationship. It's been years but there's still something between them. "What do you want to know?"

"You were going away for college, right? What happened?"

Ugh. Looks as though I'm going to have to go through this.

"Da's an alcoholic and a gambler. The entire fucking city of Dublin knows that. What no one knows is that for years he was in a lot of debt, and as he didn't have a job, Ma had to pay it." I bring my knees to my chest. "Ma had enough. She was pissed, and they fought. Da was a fucking bastard, so she upped and left."

He nods, seemingly understanding what I'm

getting at. "So your mam left, leaving you to not only pay everything off, but look after the kids too?"

"Yup. So I'm doing the best I can. I'm a whore, apparently, and deserve to pay the debt off."

He shakes his head and grimaces. "The fuck? Who called you a whore?"

"Da. He found out I'm working at the strip club and is pissed about it. I don't care. He's a fucking bastard. He's not allowed back in the house and he won't take the kids because he knows he'll have to pay for everything and have to actually care for them. So as long as I pay the debt off, he stays the fuck away from me and the children."

"It's fucked up is what it is, Ailbhe. Your da's a cunt."

"Yup, you'll have no arguments from me. He's an absolute cunt. But again, as long as he leaves me the hell alone, I don't give a fuck."

He glances toward the staircase and I brace for what he's going to say next. "What did your da promise Jed?"

Ah, no, we're not getting into that. No fucking way. "I don't know what you mean?" I lie, hoping he won't press the issue.

"Does Ruairi know what's going on?"

"Yeah, he's home and he's helping me out. But I

don't understand what you mean about what Da's promised Jed?"

He watches me carefully, almost as though he's trying to figure me out. He shakes his head. "Nothing, don't worry. Just be careful, okay? Jed's not someone you want to mess around with. Just be cautious."

I give him a soft smile. "I always am."

"Maverick and I will be around the club. We're going to ensure that you're safe."

I shake my head. Christ, that's the last thing I need. "The Fury Vipers always ensure that we're safe leaving. There's always someone around making sure we're not alone when we go home. You don't have to go out of your way to do that."

He's silent for a moment. "Ruairi's a friend, Ailbhe. I'll do anything for my friends."

"I appreciate that, but honestly, as I said, we're always monitored." I also don't want Preacher finding out what the hell is going on. That man has been even more distant than ever lately and I'm not sure why. Whenever I try to brooch the subject, I get ignored or grunted at. I know Preacher doesn't want anything but sex, but sometimes I feel as though I'm just a vessel for him to fuck whenever he gets the urge.

"You have any trouble, Ailbhe, you call me and we'll do whatever we can to help."

"I will. Thanks." I know there's no way in hell that

I'll call him. I just don't have it in me to do that. When times get tough, I only lean on myself. That's the way it's always been and I have no expectations for it to change.

We say goodbye and he leaves. I'm a little rattled by his words. I'm wondering who the hell he's been talking to. He knows a lot more than he should and that's terrifying.

Fuck. This is the very last thing I need.

"Babe," Preacher growls as I exit the club.

He showed up an hour before closing and watched me. His eyes never left me as I danced. It's such a heady feeling to have his entire focus on me. It was hard, but I had to push him from my mind and focus on the job at hand.

"Hey, Preach," I reply with a smile as I step out toward him. It's not too bad this evening. The days aren't as cold as they have been and thankfully there's no rain. Everyone's leaving and it won't be long until it's just him and I left here. "You okay?"

His gaze moves over my face. "Yeah, I'm good, babe. Are you busy tonight?"

Ah, he wants to hook up. Right now, that's not something I'm ready to do. We need to speak, not have sex. Not tonight anyway. I glance around and see Theresa's locking up, which means everyone's left.

"Do you have a minute?" I ask a little hesitantly. I'm scared. I have no idea how he's going to take it.

His brows furrow. "Sure, what's up?"

I bite my lip as I look at him. He's watching me, waiting for me to speak. I'm going to drop this bomb on him and I have no idea how he's going to react.

"Okay," I say quickly as a breath rushes out of me. "So, I need you to know that I don't want this to change things. I don't need you to do anything."

"What the fuck are you talkin' about, babe?"

I swallow hard as I wring my hands together. "I'm pregnant."

"The fuck you are," he hisses. "No the fuck you're not."

"I am," I reply, my hands trembling. I clasp them together, trying not to show the fear I'm feeling. "I'm six weeks along."

His eyes flash with anger. "I've always used protection," he snarls. "There's no way you're pregnant."

Pain lances through my heart and I sigh. God, why is he calling me a liar? There have been a few times he hasn't used a condom. "Why would I lie to you, Preacher? I mean, what the hell would I get out of doing so?"

His lip is curled in disgust. "I don't know, and I

don't give a fuck. Whatever game you're fuckin' playin', Ailbhe, I want no part in it."

"Okay," I say, my heart breaking at his words. I don't understand why he's being so callous. Sure, I knew he wouldn't be best pleased about it, but this is ridiculous.

His eyes narrow. "Fuckin' games," he snaps. The anger in his voice is like a whip, and it causes me to shiver in fear. I've never heard him like this. I don't think I've ever heard someone have so much anger in their voice before. "I don't play that shit, bitch. I won't be played. So do me a favor and get the fuck away from me, yeah? We're done. Never fuckin' come near me again."

Tears sting the back of my eyes. God, he's killing me. He's actually killing me right now. I can't believe he's acting this way. I never expected him to be this mean. "Okay, Preacher, you've got it."

I turn on my heel and walk quickly to my car, my tears falling thick and fast. I'm hurt. God, I'm so fucking hurt. He's such an arsehole. I should have known better. I should have realized that when he said he just wanted to fuck, that's all he wanted, and none of the consequences. But the truth of the matter is, he didn't always use contraception and sometimes shit happens. I just wish he'd be an adult about it all.

My tears fall the entire journey home. I have to pull

over a few times as I can't see. When I pull into the driveway of the house, I'm surprised to see lights on. Ruairi must still be awake, something that doesn't usually happen. He's always in his room and I don't bother him when I come home. Right now, I don't have it in me to care why he's still awake, nor do I want to have the added drama to my life. Ruairi's up to something, I know he is, I just don't want to know what it is. Sometimes, ignorance is bliss.

"What's wrong?" Ruairi asks as I walk into the house. "No lies, Ailbhe. You've been crying, so what happened?"

I sink down onto the sofa beside him, kicking off my shoes and bringing my knees to my chest. I can't stop the tears from falling as I tell him what happened.

"Christ, he's a fucking bastard, Al. You're better off without him. Fuck that prick."

I laugh through the sobs. "I just don't understand why he's so angry or how he could be so callous toward me. I never intended on getting pregnant, nor did I set out to trap him."

"He's a fucking bastard, Al. You don't need him. You've proven you're more than capable of taking care of children without help. You're already a good ma, Al. You're going to be fine being a single parent. Don't cry. That bastard doesn't deserve your tears."

I wipe my face, trying to swipe away the tears, but

they just keep coming. "I know. I'm just hurt. I stupidly thought he cared about me. That's my fault. I thought there was more than there was between us." I sigh. "We both know what it's like to have shitty parents, and I never wanted that for my children. Hell, I hadn't planned on having any for a while."

"Plans don't always go to plan. You know that more than anyone. But you're pregnant, Ailbhe. You have time to decide what's the best option for you."

"I've been non-stop thinking about it since I found out I was pregnant. I want to keep the baby. I want to be his or hers ma. I think I'll be able to love and provide for him or her, and that they'll be happy."

He reaches for my hand. "They will be, Al. Trust me, you'll love that baby like no one else could. It's all going to be okay. I promise you, no matter what, it's going to be okay."

I nod. He's right, it will be okay. It has to be.

"Have you eaten?" he asks.

The mere thought has my stomach protesting. I haven't eaten much since the sickness kicked in. Not only is it coming every morning, it comes every time I want to eat or drink. I'm throwing up every time I smell or think about food or drink. It's not great. I feel weaker than ever and I need it to stop. I need my strength for work.

"Let me make you some toast," Ruairi tells me. "You

need to eat something. If you don't, you're going to end up in the hospital."

I lean back against the sofa as my stomach rolls. God, I feel like shit and I'm not sure if this feeling is ever going to go away. I pray it does.

I close my eyes as Ruairi gets up from the sofa and moves toward the kitchen. I'm grateful he's here and helping me. I'm lucky to have a great family around me. Not only will my baby have me, but they'll have this amazing family too. My baby is going to be so loved.

Fuck Preacher. He can go fuck himself. He'll realize what he's missing eventually and will come crawling back. Our child is a miracle and deserves so much love from their father. So I hope he does see what he's missing and realizes his child needs him.

But from his reaction today, I don't know if that's going to happen.

CHAPTER 14
PREACHER

I stare at the bottle of whiskey in front of me. I've been good. I've stayed the fuck away from booze for a long time, and right now, I'm struggling.

Pregnant.

Ailbhe's words continue to spin around in my head. The fuck am I going to do? I can't even think straight right now. The pain that slashed through her eyes at my words is going to haunt me for a lifetime. She looked at me as though I stabbed her in the heart and ripped it from her chest.

Hearing her tell me she's pregnant brought a slew of fucking memories back. They all hit me like a ton of bricks all at once and I lashed out. I needed to take a step back and I needed Ailbhe to leave me alone for a moment. But I feel like shit. I lashed out at her and I shouldn't have, but fuck, I couldn't hold it in.

"What's goin' on, brother?" Wrath asks as he slides onto the stool beside me. "You're lookin' at that bottle as though you want to drink it all without takin' a breath."

"Got shit on my mind," I say. My words are rough, and I know that I must look like a crazed asshole. "Don't need company right now, Wrath. I've got a lot of respect for you, brother, a fuckin' lot of respect, but I need you to leave me be."

I know myself, and when I get into moods like this, I should be alone. I shouldn't be let around people because I can't hold back the anger. I'll let loose and could end up hurting someone.

"I'm a big boy, Preach. I've known you for a long fuckin' time. I may not be as close to you as Reaper was, but I'm the closest thing you've got right now."

"Appreciate that," I say thickly. "But trust me, right now, you don't want to be around me."

"What's goin' on, brother. What's happened?"

"A fuckin' lot," I hiss. "I fucked up. I think I've fucked up huge."

"How about you tell me what's happened and then I could help you?"

I shake my head. "I don't know about that, bro. I really don't want to talk about it."

He drums his fingers against the table. "Alright, I respect that, but I'm goin' to talk and take a stab at what's happened, and if I'm close, maybe you can tell me the rest, yeah?"

I don't answer him. I doubt he'll know what the fuck's going on but I let him have at it.

"You've not spoken to Reaper, so that's out. You have spoken to Esme, somethin' I'm proud of you for, brother. She's a good woman and she loves Reaper and Tyson."

"Wrath—" I warn. I don't want to fight my brother, but I fucking will.

"He's doin' good, brother. Just thought I'd let you know that. He's doin' real good, but he misses you."

I miss my kid. I fucking miss my kid so fucking much, but I did the right thing. I left him behind no matter how fucking much it hurt me. I left him with his parents and he's thriving now.

"But this is about your girl, Ailbhe," he says, and I grind my teeth. Fuck. I don't want to talk about it, and no matter how much I tell him, he's not listening to me. He's just going to continue with the bullshit. Christ, he's a fucking asshole.

"It is. Look at how pissed you are at me for talkin' about her. So what happened? You fucked up with her, that's obvious. But the question is: what did you do?"

"Leave it," I hiss.

"What happened, brother? Why the hell are you wantin' to drown yourself in alcohol?"

"Wrath," I grunt. "Seriously, fuckin' leave it."

"She tell you she don't want to see you anymore?" he asks. "I wouldn't blame her. I mean, you're a crazed motherfucker."

My lips twitch. "Probably she won't anymore."

He winces. "Christ, what did you do?"

He's not going to shut the hell up. I reach for the bottle and get to my feet.

"She's pregnant," I snarl. "That is what happened. She's pregnant and I lost my shit. She's not goin' to want to fuckin' see me again. Wrath, you tell that to another soul, and me and you are goin' to have problems."

He holds up his hands. "Won't say a word, but fuck, brother, what are you gonna do?"

I shake my head. "Nothin'. What the fuck am I supposed to do? I mean, I've already been down this road. I ain't goin' to do it again. No fuckin' way."

He nods, unable to say anything. "I get that, brother, but Ailbhe isn't Pepper. This is a different situation to that. You and I both know that your girl is fucking sweet as hell."

I scrub a hand down my face. "I know, but it still doesn't change the fact that I've been down that road before and I won't be doing it again."

"Alright, brother, I get you. But you need anythin', just let me know."

"Keep an eye on Ailbhe," I ask him. "I need you to do that for me, brother. I need you to ensure that she's safe."

"You don't ever have to ask me that," he promises me. "I'll sort it out. I'll make sure I'm at the club when Ailbhe is and ensure that she's safe."

I nod. "I appreciate that. Thanks, Wrath. But I'm askin' you, don't tell anyone else about this."

I've got my own guilt to deal with. Knowing I've fucked up is a bitter pill to swallow, but there's nothing I can do. I need Wrath's help in keeping Ailbhe safe, but everyone else needs to keep the fuck out of this shit. I can't deal with everyone else knowing. Not right now. I know that if the women find out about what's going on with me and Ailbhe, they'll be all up in Ailbhe's business and she doesn't need that. She's fucking pregnant and she doesn't need to have bullshit on her shoulders.

I take my bottle and move toward my room. Tonight, I'm going to drown my fucking guilt in this bottle of whiskey and enjoy every fucking sip of it. I'll finally have a good night's sleep without having dreams. I'll drink until I pass the fuck out.

"Yo, Preach," I hear Mayhem call out, his voice filled with anger. That's not something new. The guy's always pissed about something, but there's an added edge to it now and I'm not sure what the fuck is going on.

I look up at him and see the rage bubbling in his eyes. "What?"

"You got a minute? Need to talk to you, brother," May says, his eyes focused solely on me.

A tingling sensation makes it along my spine. Right now, I'm not in the mood for whatever bullshit this is about.

"Brother, whatever you've got to say, you can say now. We're celebratin'," I tell him. We've found out that Serenity and Shadow are having a girl.

May shakes his head. "Trust me, Preach, this needs to be said in private."

"How about you say whatever it is now, May?" Ace says, a little unease in his voice.

The prez has spoken, and May grinds his teeth. "Fuck, I wanted to do this in private," he snarls. *"When you were shot, Effie realized that your blood type is O Positive."*

I shrug. I know what my blood type is. "Yeah, what of it?"

"You know that Tyson's blood type is AB, right?" Mayhem asks.

There are a lot of murmurs going around the clubhouse, a lot of anger too.

"Someone want to tell me what the fuck is goin' on?" I snarl, pissed at the situation. What the fuck is going on?

"A parent with the blood type O Positive," May begins, "can't be the parent of a child with the blood type of AB."

The room is stunned to silence. I hear the women crying, and I feel my brothers' anger whipping around the room and clogging the air.

"What the fuck you sayin', May?" I growl, trying to comprehend what the fuck he's just said.

"I'm sorry, brother, but there's no possible way that Tyson is yours biologically."

Pain lances through my heart at his word. I'm finding it hard to breathe. What the fuck? Everything starts to make sense, and the words Pepper used to say ring in my ears.

"He's not yours," she used to taunt. I used to think it was just to piss me off, but it's true.

Fucking Pepper. That Goddamn bitch. She's fucking up my boy's life even from beyond the grave.

A few days later

I hold my boy tight and keep him close to my chest, even though my heart is beating a mile a minute. The thought of leaving him kills me. I can't be without him. He's my son. I don't give a fuck what the biology says. I don't give a fuck what the results say. Tyson is my son. I'm the one who has kept him alive his entire life and now someone else is going to raise him as their own. I can't fucking breathe at the thought.

Tyson coos in my arms, his silverish eyes looking up at me with such happiness. Fuck. Why is this shit happening to me? Why on earth did Pepper play me so fucking badly?

Losing Abel and then sinking into that dark place was hard. I wrecked so many lives due to how the fuck my past affected me. My parents fucked me up and then losing my brother was the hardest thing in my life, or so I thought. But nothing compares to how I am feeling right now. Losing my son is by far the deepest pain I'll ever feel. But I'll be damned if I'm going to give him up without a fight. Tyson is my son. I'll make sure that I won't leave him.

I won't be leaving him. I will take him and fucking run. No fucking doubt about it, I'll run. I'll live the nomad life with my boy.

Once I'm finished packing, Tyson's fast asleep in my arms. I sink down onto the bed and hold him tighter. Tears fall from my eyes and I'm unable to stop them.

What the fuck is going to happen now?

Fourteen hours later

Finding out that Reaper is Tyson's father was the biggest blow I could have been given. Anyone else, and I was running. I didn't give a fuck. I would have taken my boy and ran. But I couldn't do that to Reaper. I've taken so much from him already. He served time for me; I couldn't take my boy from him too.

No matter how hard Reaper tried to make me stay, tried to explain that he would keep things as they were, that I could still be Tyson's dad, I couldn't do it. I couldn't live with him in the compound knowing that I'm taking the opportunity to be a father away from him. That's not who I am and it's not something I would have ever been able to do. Anyone else and I was gone, but not Reaper. Never to him.

"Ladies and Gentlemen, we're thirty minutes away from landing. The weather in Dublin is three degrees Celsius with light showers," the captain says over the intercom.

Once my mind was made up there was no changing it. I had to leave, and going Nomad wasn't the option for me yet. I needed to be around my brothers. I know that if I'm alone, I'm sinking to the deepest and darkest part of my mind and soul. There wouldn't be any way out. I wouldn't be able to pull myself out.

The plane lands, and I'm grateful to be out in the open air. While the weather is wet, the fresh air hits my lungs and I breathe in deeply.

Can I start over here for a while? Time will tell.

But fuck, this pain in my chest is tight and I don't think that I'll ever be able to get rid of it. It's from losing Tyson and that feeling isn't ever going to go away.

Fuck.

I pray that my son is going to be okay. I know he'll be loved and cared for, but Christ, I'm going to miss him like fuck. The thought of not being with him tears me apart.

I never thought I'd lose him, but sometimes life has other plans for you.

God, if Pepper was still alive, I'd slit her throat and watch as the bitch struggled to breathe. I would smile as the life left her eyes. She got away with her sins far too fucking easily.

The day I die, I'll be happy. It means I get to see that cunt Pepper again and I'll finally get revenge for all the hurt that bitch has laid on everyone.

CHAPTER 15
AILBHE

"He's not here again, girl," Tamara tells me. "He's a fucking dick. You're better off without him."

I sigh. It's been two weeks and I haven't seen Preacher since I told him I was pregnant. I'm so stupid. After I told him I was pregnant, I went home sobbing, but when I woke the next morning, I thought it would take a couple of days and then he'd reach out and talk to me. But that hasn't been the case. Instead, he's hiding. He's no longer coming to the club. That hurts, because I know it's because of me that he's not here. I'm so stupid. I should have known better. I should never have gotten my hopes up and I shouldn't have believed that he'd change his mind. He made his feelings known and I should have taken him at his word. Instead, I got my hopes up, and that's on me.

"Look, there's nothing I can do about it," I tell her honestly. "Whatever happens, happens. We had fun and it's over now."

"Yeah, but you've got to live with the consequences of that fun while he gets to walk away without a care in the world. It's utter bullshit. So fucked up."

I wave my hand in dismissal. "We never promised each other anything. It is what it is and I'm not going to beg him to listen to me. He's made his decision and it's up to him to make the first move if he wants to change his mind."

"Bullshit," she fires back. "You and I both know if he came back to you now, you'd be jumping all over his dick."

I laugh. She's so eloquent. "Whatever. Now, we've got to get ready and get out there." I rise to my feet and reach for the hairbrush, but I stumble as I reach for it.

"Woah," she says, rushing toward me. "Are you still not eating or drinking properly?"

I sigh. "Nope," I say as I take a seat again. "I just haven't been able to keep anything down. Whenever I think I'm feeling a little better, it hits me like a ton of bricks and I'm on my knees throwing everything up."

She rubs circles on my back. "It's going to be okay," she promises me. "You've got a few more dances and then you're off for two days. Maybe call the doctor and see if there's anything they can give you."

I lean my head backwards. "Sounds like a plan," I say. "I'm sick of being told that it's normal and a good sign for the baby. Well I say screw that as it's not good for me."

She laughs. "That's true, it's not good for you. You're pale—"

I glare at her. "I'm always pale."

"Well, paler than usual. You're barely able to stay on your feet. You need to figure something out, girl. Otherwise you're going to end up in the hospital."

"I promise I'll call the doctors in the morning and make an appointment." I'm hoping Tamara's right and I'll be able to get something to help me ease the sickness.

She presses a kiss to my cheek. "Good. Now, let me help you get ready. You need to take sips of water, little sips."

I reach for my bottle and take the tiniest of sips, but as usual, my stomach cramps and a wave of heat passes over me.

"Are you sure you're going to be okay?" she asks.

"I'll be fine," I assure her. "It'll pass in a second."

But as always it doesn't. Heat washes over me as nausea hits me. I get to my feet and make a mad dash to the bathroom. Thankfully, I make it in time. My stomach cramps as I vomit. God, will this ever end?

"Al, are you okay?" Tamara calls out.

"Yep," I say a little too weakly. "I'll be out in a minute." My entire body is shaken. I have little to no energy, but I have to push through it all. I have bills to pay, and if I don't have the money for Jed tomorrow, there will be hell to pay. The very last thing I need on top of this is to have that man on my back. Not again.

It takes me a few minutes to stand. I'm still shaky but I'm able to move. I'm not surprised to find Tamara waiting for me when I exit the bathroom. "You're not fine."

"I will be. It's just a few more hours. I can do that." I've been doing it every day since this started. "I'll be okay."

She gives me a look that tells me she doesn't believe me. There's not much we can do. I'm just going to have to suck it up and continue with my day.

"Have you tried something different? What about sparkling water? The bubbles could help? Well, that's what my mam said anyway."

I recoil in horror. "That shouldn't be a thing," I say in disgust. "I think that would make me vomit even more."

She laughs. "You won't know until you try." She goes to her bag and pulls out a bottle. "I always keep a bottle in my bag. While you may not like it, it really helps me. It quenches my thirst like no other."

I take it from her, and open the bottle, I hear the

hiss, I'm not hopeful that it'll help. "Thank you." As I take a sip, the bubbles hit my nose, but I swallow it down. Just as the last time, my stomach recoils.

"Oh crap," Tamara says as I make a dash to the bathroom. "I thought for sure it could help."

It takes me a little longer this time to recover. When I get out of the bathroom, she's waiting with a soft smile. "Christ, Ailbhe, I'm sorry."

I shake my head. "Not your fault."

She gives me a mock scowl. "No, it's Preacher's fault. He's the one who should be taking care of you."

I roll my eyes. We're not getting into this. "We'd better get out there. You're up on stage soon."

She flashes me a smile. "That I am. It's a packed crowd out there, which means loads of money for us."

Here's hoping. I'd like to pay Jed more money this week. I've had a good week. Not to mention, with Ruairi chipping in, I've been able to save a lot more to put away. I'm hoping this debt will go down and I won't have to worry about him and his sleazy threats. There's nothing worse than listening to him threaten to rape me if I don't pay up.

I make my way around the floor. Punters are flashing their cash, getting all the girls' attention. Tamara wasn't wrong, it is a packed crowd, and they're all eager to spend their money. Most of them want lap dances. That's something that's easy to do and I get a decent amount of tips for. Obviously my dance on the pole brings in the most money.

"Christ," Lorna says under her breath as we take a quick breather. Lorna started working here last week and I love her already. She's sweet but she's not a pushover. She's fun and someone that Tamara, Kelsie, and I can hang out with. "Why is it so busy?"

I shake my head. "I've no idea. It's beyond crazy tonight." I'm drained. I can feel it in my bones. I don't have much energy left, and I don't want to risk having another sip of water. If I do, I know I'm going to throw up, and that's just going to cause even more exhaustion, something I can't afford right now. I need to make it through the night and then I can collapse once I'm home and in bed.

"But the tips are great." She grins. "Where's Kelsie?" she asks. "I haven't seen her at all this week. Does she still work here?"

"You know Kelsie?" I question, surprised as Kelsie is in the middle of her exams and has taken the past month off. She'll be back next week, and she's excited as she'll be able to start saving for a home.

"She's my sister's friend. It's how I got the job."

Ah, she must be Dara's sister. I've heard a lot about Dara. "Ah, okay. Yeah, she still works here. She should be back next week."

She gives me a brighter grin than before. "Okay,

cool." We hear a loud cheer, and Lorna's eyes widen. "We'd better get back out there. No doubt they'll start to riot if not."

I laugh. She's right, there aren't enough girls working the floor tonight to deal with the amount of people wanting lap dances. I watch as she leaves and take just a few more moments to catch my breath and try to stop the exhaustion from setting in even more.

My legs are wobbly as I move back onto the floor.

"Yo, Al, you're up on stage next. Are you ready?" Tamara calls out, and I smile.

I'm ready. Just two more dances and a few more hours. I'm almost at the end. Not much longer to go.

A few minutes later, the music begins and my body starts to sway. It doesn't take long until I'm fully into the dance. As always, I flash a smile every so often as my gaze moves across the crowd that's watching. It always helps to make them feel as though I'm giving them that secret smile, which improves my tips.

The dance is close to the end when I feel that wave of heat hit me. I will the nausea to not come, but before I can do anything, my legs start to tremble even more, my eyes blur, and my mind goes blank. I hear someone calling my name as I hit the floor, no longer having the strength to hold my body up. Just as I hit the floor, the darkness pulls me under, and the last thing I remember is praying that my baby is okay.

CHAPTER 16
PREACHER

I sit up in bed at the sound of the door banging against the wall. My eyes try to adjust to the bright light. "The fuck?" I growl, as I turn to the sound of the noise.

"The fuck is right," Pyro snarls. "Thought we agreed, brother?"

My head is pounding. It's like a continuous thumping against my temple. I wince as the loudness of his voice does nothing to ease the pain.

"What'cha talkin' about?" I say, my words slurred.

He stalks toward the bed. "This," he hisses as he grabs the bottle of whiskey. "Thought we had a deal?"

"We did," I snap, pissed that he's all up in my face. "That deal ended. What's it got to do with you?"

His lip curls in disgust. "You know, Preach, I had a fuckin' lot of respect for you. You're my brother, and you've more than earned it. But there are times when I do wonder about you. The shit you've been through, it changes a man. I wasn't sure how you'd deal with not havin' Tyson, but, brother, you showed everyone just how fuckin' tough you are. It would have brought most men to their knees. Not you. It turned you to drink. That's understandable. I finally thought you'd come out the other end and then you do this."

He's right. I turned to alcohol to numb the pain. The pain that could easily bring me to my knees and on occasion has almost done just that. But he doesn't get to judge me. Fuck no. I've done what the fuck I've needed to do in order to stay sane. Fuck him.

"You don't want to go there, Py. You really don't want to fuckin' go there with me."

"Yeah? You think you're hurtin' and that you're the only one that's doin' so? This bullshit that you're pushin' on that innocent girl, that you're not good enough for her? The one that was just fun for you?"

I push up off the bed, my legs uneasy. I'm still a little drunk from last night. "Don't fuckin' talk about her."

He shakes his head. "Nah, brother, that's exactly what we're goin' to fuckin' talk about. You see, that girl, that fuckin' sweet and innocent girl, doesn't deserve your bullshit."

"You think I don't know that?" I snarl. "You think I

haven't thought the exact same thing, that I don't think it twenty times a fuckin' day. Ailbhe is probably the purest, sweetest thing ever, and I'm not goin' to fuck her up, Py. I won't do that to her."

"Bit late, wouldn't you say?"

His words hit me. "Fuckin' Wrath. I fuckin' warned him. That motherfucker."

"Wrath didn't say shit, brother. You see, last night, we all noticed that Ailbhe wasn't herself. She's lost weight, and she looks sick, but we kept an eye on her and let her do her thing."

His words are like a punch in the gut. I haven't seen her in two weeks. I hadn't noticed she'd lost weight.

"She was up on the pole last night, Preacher. She fuckin' collapsed on stage."

Blood rushes to my head and the pounding intensifies. There's a ringing in my ears. "What?" I hiss. "The fuck did you say?"

"She collapsed. I was there, brother. I was workin' last night. I called the ambulance for her, and imagine my fuckin' surprise when her friend told the paramedic Ailbhe's pregnant."

My pulse races as sweat beads across my forehead. Fuck. I've done this. I should have protected her, stayed with her, made sure she was okay.

"Where is she?" I demand. I need to know where she is. I need to know she's okay.

"I ain't tellin' you. Not in that fuckin' state. You can barely fuckin' stand as it is."

I run a hand through my hair. Fuck, he's right. "Is she okay?"

He shakes his head. "I stayed with her last night. I learned a fuckin' lot about your woman last night, Preach. None of which she wants you to know. I was in fuckin' awe listenin' to her. But truth of the matter is, she's far from fuckin' okay. She's dehydrated. The pregnancy is rough, and she hasn't been able to eat or drink. Anytime she does, she's pukin' her fuckin' guts up. She's had no energy, and whenever she leaves work she's collapsing on the bed and sleepin'."

Fuck... How the hell did I not know this? Why the fuck didn't I know what's been going on?

I didn't want to. That's why. I didn't care to fucking know. The moment she told me she was pregnant, I ceased to fucking care about anything other than getting the fuck away from her.

"Why the hell is she workin' if she's so sick?"

He snarls at me. "That's her story, not mine. But she truly is pregnant, brother. That's your fuckin' kid she's carryin' and you're fuckin' it all up because of what that cunt Pepper did to you. You've got to realize that she's not Pepper and that you've got a child who'll be here in the next seven months or so. You'd better get your head around it sooner or later. Otherwise, you're gonna be without another child."

I sink down onto my bed and bury my head in my hands. He's right. I need to sort my fuckin' shit out. The question is: how the fuck do I do that? I can't see fucking straight when it comes to her. The pain of losing Tyson is holding me back from Ailbhe and the baby.

"How do we know it's mine?" I ask, and the moment the words leave my lips, I wince. Pyro's right, Ailbhe isn't Pepper and there's no way she'd do that to me. But fuck, the fear is rooted so deeply within my veins that I can't see anything else.

"Preach," he says low. "Did you say that to her? You don't look surprised that she's pregnant."

"She told me," I reply. "I didn't outright ask her, but I did call her a liar and basically told her to stay the fuck away from me."

Silence fills the room. "Damn, brother." He releases a low whistle. "That's some fucked up thing to say to a woman who's just told you she's pregnant with your kid. Fuckin' Pepper really fucked you up."

I glance at him. "If the tables were turned, brother, don't you think you'd be just as fucked up?"

He nods. "Yeah, I probably would be. So what are you goin' to do about Ailbhe?"

I lift my shoulders and shrug. I've no fucking idea. Can I even fix things between us?

"First place to start is to get a shower, then some food, maybe even some coffee. Then you can go and see her."

I raise a brow. "She at the hospital?"

He shakes his head. "Nah, she pitched a fit and was let out first thing this morning. She returned home with the promise that she'd rest up."

Well, that's exactly where I plan on heading once I've showered.

I hear Pyro's chuckle as I move toward the bathroom. "What?"

"You have no idea where she lives, do you?"

My feet stumble and I reach out for the chair to hold on to. "Fuck," I hiss. He's right. I have no fucking idea where she lives.

"Get a shower, brother. Once you've eaten, I'll take you to her. But best be warned, Chloe and her mom are on the warpath. Something about Ailbhe's brother being Freddie's friend or some shit."

Great, just what I fucking need. More women who are crazy angry with me.

"Thanks for the heads up," I sigh.

Once I'm in the bathroom, I hear my bedroom door close and I begin to strip out of my clothes.

I've no doubt got an uphill battle. I've fucked up

with Ailbhe, and I don't know if there's any coming back from it, but I'll do my very best to try. I'm not sure how we're going to get around it all. I've hurt her, there's no denying that, but can I mend things?

Fuck, I don't even want to think about the baby. I can't do that. If it turns out to be the exact same as it was with Tyson, I'll lose my ever-loving shit. I wouldn't be able to go through that again. No fucking way.

I'm straddling my bike as I'm parked outside of a terraced house. It's smaller than most American homes. No one is home, or if they are, they're ignoring me and Pyro.

"Who the fuck are you?" I hear growled from behind me. "And why the hell are you parked outside of my house?"

I turn and see a guy in his mid-twenties staring at Pyro and me. He's wearing a white t-shirt that shows off his muscles and a pair of jeans. He's got four kids with him; three girls, and a teenage boy.

"Your house?" Pyro asks. "Pretty sure this is Ailbhe's house. It was when I dropped her off this mornin'."

"Ah, you must be Pyro," the guy says, stepping forward. "Thanks for taking care of her. She told me you stayed with her all night. I appreciate that."

"And you are?" I ask, unable to contain the snarl.

"Who the fuck are you?" the guy fires back.

"I'm having a guess," the oldest of the girls say. "That he's Ailbhe's baby daddy."

"What's a baby daddy?" the youngest of the girls asks.

"Wait," the middle girl says, "Ailbhe's having a baby?"

"Nicely done, Fi," the teenager hisses as he picks up the youngest girl, who's sobbing. "Now you've upset Evie."

"Why are you crying?" Fi asks the young girl. "It's going to be so cool to be aunties."

"But I wanted Ailbhe to be my mammy."

"How about we talk inside?" I hear, and my heart races as I turn and see Ailbhe standing in the doorway holding the door open.

The youngest girl wiggles from the teenager's arms, and the moment her feet hit the ground she's rushing toward Ailbhe. I watch as my girl scoops up the youngster and holds her close, whispering to her.

"You're meant to be resting," the big guy tells her.

"Ruairi," Ailbhe says, sounding exasperated. "Not now."

Ah, so this is her brother, and I'm guessing the other children are also her siblings. But then that begs the question as to why the youngest would want

Ailbhe to be her mom? Christ, I have a lot of questions that need answering.

I get off my bike and move toward the house. Ailbhe's eyes narrow as she watches me move toward her. Thankfully, she doesn't tell me to leave. She'd have every right to do that, but fuck, it's good that she's not.

"Ailbhe, is he your boyfriend?" the little girl in her arms asks her with a big, wide smile.

"No, Evie, not at all. This is Preacher. He's one of my bosses."

I'm a fuck of a lot more than that. For her to say that I'm just her boss is like a fucking knife to the gut. She's bloody killing me.

"But you're having a baby?" Evie asks.

"Yeah, honey, I am," Ailbhe says softly. "That's not going to change how much I love you."

The little girl grins widely. "You're the best," she says, pressing a kiss to Ailbhe's cheek.

"Ailbhe," Ruairi growls. "Go sit down. You need to rest. You're not long home from the hospital. You need to take it easy." He pushes past me and takes the little girl from Ailbhe's arms, leaving both Ailbhe and I alone at the door.

"What are you doing here, Preacher? You made your feelings pretty clear to me when I told you about the pregnancy." The sorrow in her voice is yet another slice to my heart. I knew she'd be pissed and hurt, but hearing the pain that I've caused is worse than I could have ever imagined.

"You've been sick," I say.

She raises a brow as she leans against the doorframe. "So I have, but that doesn't explain why you're here."

I run a hand over my face. "I'm sorry," I tell her. "I truly am fuckin' sorry. I never intended to hurt you."

"You were callous, Preacher. I never asked you to do anything or to be involved. You called me a liar," she whispers, tears pooling in her eyes. "You are a dickhead, Preacher, and honestly, I don't really care what you do as long as you do it away from me."

That's never going to happen. She has no idea just how much I want her. The fucked up shit that has happened to me shaped who I am and the reactions that I have. "I needed space—"

Her laugh is mirthless. "Take all the space you want," she says angrily. "Take as long as you want. Just don't come here. I don't want anything to do with you anymore. Once the baby is born, I won't stop you from seeing him or her, but I don't want any type of relationship with you other than you being the father of my child."

She's dead serious. She's not wavering from this. I've got a lot of groveling to do to make up for this. But I need to know that the baby is mine.

"Inside, Ailbhe," Ruairi growls. "You need to sit down on the sofa and rest."

She sighs but does as her brother tells her. I follow her into the house, and I'm shocked to find all of her siblings sitting around the sitting room waiting for her.

"What's going on, Ailbhe?" her sister Fiona asks her. "Who is he and why is he here?"

Ailbhe sighs. "This is Preacher."

"He's the sperm donor," her younger brother says with a grin.

I hear Pyro cough but I don't turn. I already know the asshole is covering up his laughter. "Damn, bro, you've really fucked up."

"What's a sperm donor?" Evie asks, and that sets Pyro off. The fucker chuckles out loud, which has the kids laughing.

"It doesn't matter, honey. He's not staying. He's going now," Ailbhe tells her as she strokes her hair. "How was school?"

"Good. Fiadh played with me all day."

"That's great, honey. I'm glad you had a good day. Now, I need you and your brother and sisters to go and do your homework."

All the kids get to their feet and do exactly as Ailbhe tells them. "Ruairi will help you, Evie."

"I'll help in a bit, Ev. I want to know what the hell this dick wants."

"Ruairi," Ailbhe hisses. "Language around Evie."

"Why is he here?" Ruairi snaps as he turns to me. "Why?"

"I want to talk with Ailbhe."

"Speak then, Yank," he growls.

"Hey," Ailbhe cries. "Don't do that, Ruairi."

Her brother shrugs as he continues to glare at me.

"Preacher, whatever it is you have to say, please just say it so you can go," Ailbhe says on a sigh.

I return the glare to her brother and then focus on Ailbhe. "I know I fucked up. But there's a reason for it—"

"What's the reason?" she asks me. "I'd like to know what the reason is."

I shake my head. I'm not getting into that, not now, hell not fucking ever. "Not here to discuss that right now, Ailbhe."

Her eyes are narrowed as she glares at me. "Then why are you here?" I watch as she takes a deep breath. "You said you wanted to talk. So tell me what the hell it is you want to say."

I try to find a way to say the words gently, but they just tumble out of my mouth. "I want a paternity test."

Silence spreads through the room, and I know that I've fucked up. I hadn't meant to outright ask it like that. Christ, I'm a fucking asshole. There's no fucking doubt about that.

"I'll get you the paternity test," Ailbhe says, her words vibrating with anger and sadness. "But I don't need you to raise this baby. I don't want you anywhere near me. What I do want is for you to go sit on a fucking cactus and go fuck yourself."

I hear Pyro's chuckle and sigh. I really did fuck this up. Damn it.

"It's time to go," Ruairi growls. "She's supposed to be resting. The last thing she needs is your fucking bullshit. So do something right, and leave her the fuck alone."

Py slams his hand on my shoulder, his fingers digging into the muscle. "Time to go, brother," he says low.

I don't want to leave. Fuck, I'm so damn stupid. I fucked up. I shouldn't have said anything about the paternity test. I should have kept my damn mouth shut.

I turn on my heel and leave, not wanting to upset her any more. She needs to rest and she needs time to calm down. Fuck, I need to find a way to make it up to her. If she gets the chance, she's going to skin me alive, and I don't blame her at fucking all.

"Brother," Pyro says, shaking his head. "Damn, brother, that was fucked up."

I nod. "I know. I fucked up. I should have kept my damn mouth shut."

"That you should have. Why did you think it was the right question to ask?"

"Fuck if I know. It was like word vomit and I couldn't stop it. She fuckin' hates me."

He chuckles. "Not that you can blame her, right? I mean, that was beyond crazy. What are you goin' to do now?"

"Fuck, I don't know how to fix this. I just tend to make everything worse. I don't know how to make amends."

"Well, you've got to, brother. The woman's carryin' your child and you truly hurt her today."

I know that, and I'm going to have to find a way to apologize to her without making things worse. Something I have a hard time doing. It just seems that I put my foot in my mouth all the damn time. One thing's for sure, I'll be making sure that Ailbhe is okay. Whatever the hell she needs, I'll make sure she has it. I don't give a fuck what it is.

CHAPTER 17
AILBHE

"You doing okay, Ailbhe?" Fiona asks me as she takes a seat beside me.

Today has been better. I'm feeling a little stronger than I have the last couple of days, but I'm still struggling to keep anything down. But the tablets the doctor gave me should work in the next couple of days. I'm praying it does because I've been feeling like shit and it needs to stop. It's been going on for way too bloody long.

"I'm okay. This baby is kicking my butt, girl," I say with a smile. "But I'm okay. I promise."

"Evie and Hannah are scared," she says softly. The girls are in bed. They've been worried since they got home from school yesterday.

"I never intended for you all to find out that way." I

hate that they found out by me being sick and ending up in the hospital.

"We were worried that you weren't home when we woke up. We had no idea you were sick. Why didn't you say something?"

I wave her away, hoping she's feeling better about it. "I didn't want to worry you all, but I should have let you know about the pregnancy. Why are the girls afraid?"

"They think that when the baby comes, you're not going to want them here anymore."

I sigh. I should have known they were afraid that the baby would make things change. "That's never going to change. I promise you, Fi, I'm never going to push you away or leave you because I have a baby."

"But things will change," she says softly, and I know that it isn't just Hannah and Evie who are worried. Fiona is too.

"They will. You won't have a good night's sleep again for a few years. There's going to be another child in the house, one that needs to be fed, changed, and looked after. But my feelings for all of you won't change. I love you all so very much, and I promise that will never change. I will always love you all." I reach for her and pull her into my arms. "Promise you, Fi, you're stuck with me forever. I'm not leaving you."

I'm not our parents. I learned a lot about who I am when they left me to raise their children. But I'm glad I was here to be the one to raise them. The kids are amazing, and watching them thrive is something I truly enjoy. I really do love each and every one of those kids and I wouldn't leave them at all. No fucking way.

"Promise?" she whispers.

I hold her tight, not wanting to let her go. "I promise, Fi, I'm here for you. Whenever you need me, I'll always be at your side."

"I love you, Al," she tells me. "So much. Thank you for looking after us."

I hold her tightly. "I wouldn't have it any other way," I assure her. "I love being here with you and the other kids. We're family, and that's something that's never going to change. You're stuck with me."

She laughs, just as I had expected her to. "You're the best. Have you thought of names for the baby?"

I release her and smile. It's so good to be able to talk with her about it. "Not yet. Honestly, I'm just trying to get through this sickness. Let me guess, you have already chosen some."

She bounces on the seat and claps her hands. "I have. I think I've chosen some really good names."

Ruairi comes into the room with a cup of tea in his hands and passes it to me. "Please drink," he tells me. "I don't want you to end up in the hospital again."

"What he means," Mikey says as he follows in behind Ruairi, "is that he doesn't want to be left with all of us again."

I smile because I have a feeling Mikey's not far off. Ruairi finds it hard to have all four kids together. He's never had to do it, and it's a scary thing to be in charge of four children. It's hard, and I love that he's done it for me while I couldn't.

"So, what's this I hear about names?" Ruairi asks with a grin.

Once again, Fiona bounces on her seat. "Okay, for a boy, I think Emmett is such a cute name. What do you think?"

I smile. I actually really love that name. I think it's for sure a contender. "Love it." I glance around and see that Ruairi and Mikey are nodding in agreement.

"Also, Kennedy?"

No, that doesn't hit the same as Emmett did.

"Okay, so that's no then," she says with a laugh. "What's Preacher's real name?"

Well now, isn't that a question? Hmm, that's something I should really know. "I've no idea. Any other suggestions?"

"Brian, Kane, Casey?"

Kane. Now that's another name I like. "Kane is good. So we have two options for a boy: Kane and

Emmett. What about a girl?" I ask her, loving how excited she is.

"Oh, I have some names for a girl too. There's Shannon, Bronagh, Aoibheann, Bláithín, and Sadhbh."

"There are a lot of Irish names on that list, Fi," Mikey says with a laugh. "But I think Sadhbh is good."

I nod. "I agree, Sadhbh or Bronagh."

She claps again, reminding me of a seal. "I can't believe I'm going to be an auntie. I'm so excited. It's going to be so much fun."

I nudge her with my foot. "It will be. Now, it's time for you to go to bed."

She sighs but doesn't lose her smile. "I'm going. I'm going. Good night, Ailbhe. Please drink the tea."

I take a sip to show her that I am trying. Thankfully, my stomach doesn't protest as it goes down. "Good night, sweet dreams."

Mikey gets to his feet. "I'm going too. I'll leave you and Ruairi to talk. No doubt you've got a lot to talk about."

I roll my eyes. He's not wrong, we do have a lot to talk about, and I have no doubt that he's going to be asking questions about Preacher and everything that happened today.

I'm so hurt by him wanting a paternity test. I knew he didn't believe me about being pregnant, but for him to think that I'd be sleeping with someone else is heartbreaking. It took everything I had not to cry. I wouldn't cry in front of him or the kids. I just wouldn't do that and make the kids worry, nor would I give him the satisfaction of seeing me cry.

"Night, Mikey," both Ruairi and I say in unison.

"Talk to me, Al. What's going on with that prick?"

I grin. Trust my brother to always make me feel better. "I don't know. Honestly, I'm a little numb. I'm hurt, so bloody hurt that he'd ever think I'd do that to anyone, let alone him. It's painful to know someone thinks about me like that."

He nods. "He fucked up. I could see that he realized he hurt you. The moment the words left his mouth, he fucked up, and he knows that."

"Still doesn't make it right," I sigh. "He doesn't know me and I don't know him. It was supposed to be fun, and that's all it was, but sometimes things happen. I never intended for this to happen. Hell, this was the last thing I needed. But it's going to be okay. I know that with everything in me. It's all going to be okay."

"It will be. Because you're tough and you'll do whatever it takes. You've proven that. But, Al, what's going to happen with Preacher?"

I glance away and take another sip of the tea. "I have no idea. I'm not vindictive. Even though he's really hurt me, I won't stop him from seeing the baby, but I do feel as though everything between us is dead."

"Can you co-parent peacefully with him?" he asks.

"Of course," I reply, affronted. "I can push my feelings aside, Ruairi."

"Then you both need to have a discussion. That man has demons, Al. You can see them every time you look at him. There's something that's happened that's made him this way. Talk with him and lay everything out."

"Do you think I should do a paternity test?" I ask him, wondering if that's the way to go.

He's silent, and that's all the answer I need. He does think it's the right thing to do. "The best thing for you all is to have it done and that way it'll put your mind at ease. It will ease the stress from you."

I laugh. I don't think that's possible at fucking all. "It's shit that I have to do this but fuck it. If it's the only thing to do, I'll do it, but I'm not sure if I could ever forgive him for doubting me."

"No one ever said you have to forgive him. You're doing what you need to do for your baby."

I groan. "I'll give it a few days, let my emotions settle, and hopefully by then the medicine the doctor gave me should have kicked in and I'll be stronger and able to keep food and drink down a lot more."

"Here's hoping," Ruairi says with a grimace. "But I think you'll feel better once it's done."

Eh, that's something I'm not so sure that will happen, but I'm going to try.

"I'll go and see him in a week or so." By then, I should be less emotional and more guarded. I won't let him hurt me again.

I just hope that he's willing to listen to what I have to say and won't try to railroad me.

CHAPTER 18
PREACHER
ONE MONTH LATER

"You look better, brother," Wrath says as he slides onto the stool beside me. "How are things with Ailbhe?"

I sigh as I look down at the floor. "Fucked up. It's worse than it has ever been. I was an asshole, brother. I fucked up and I don't think there's any going back."

"What happened? Py wouldn't tell us anythin'. All he said was that Ailbhe collapsed and hasn't been well."

"Yeah, somethin' happened. She's not been able to keep anythin' down. She's dehydrated."

"Fuck, man, is she okay?" he's worried about her, she's not been at work and Py and I haven't said anything about what's going on. I guess today he's wanting to know more.

"She's home and she's doin' okay. She's lost weight and she's weak. But that's not what's fucked up."

I hear his swift intake of breath. "Christ, brother, what did you do?"

"I asked her for a paternity test," I say low. "The look of devastation on her face will haunt me forever. Fuck, brother, I hurt her. I fuckin' hurt her so badly."

"Fuck," he hisses. "Damn, Preacher, that's fucked up. Please tell me you had a little more finesse than that?"

I chuckle. Christ, I wish I did. "No, I tried to work it through in my head, tried to figure out what I should say, but it just tumbled out, and yeah, I blurted it out."

He shakes his head. "That's a motherfuckin' uphill battle you've got to make amends."

"Tell me somethin' I don't know. It's fucked. I know she's not lyin' to me. I know deep down that she's carryin' my child. But I'm so twisted inside, Wrath, I can't function. I need to have proof. It's crazy, I get it, but fuck, I need to know that it's my child before I get attached again. I can't lose another child."

His hand lands on my shoulder and he squeezes tight. "I get it," he says low. "I really do understand where you're coming from. You've been through hell and you're scarred. You've been burned and you don't want it to happen again. You're protectin' yourself, and there's nothin' wrong with that. But the way you've gone about it is fucked up, brother, and while you're tryin' to do what's right for you, you hurt your woman along the way."

I run my hands through my hair. "I did, and that's something I'm not sure I can repair. You didn't see her face, brother. You didn't see how fuckin' hurt she was."

"You've got time, Preach. You've got time to make things right before the baby gets here."

I nod. "I do, and I plan on ensuring that everything is worked out before he or she gets here."

"How do you think it'll go down when you and Ailbhe speak?" he asks.

I groan. "Fuck, I have no idea. I'm hoping it'll go smoothly and we'll be able to talk but I'm not sure. She's hurt, and if I were in her shoes, I wouldn't want to talk to me."

"But she's not you," he laughs. "She's sweet and innocent. I doubt she'll be an asshole. I don't think she'll dismiss you."

"I hope you're right." I really do fucking hope that she's willing to let me speak.

"Will you open up to her?" he asks, and I recoil. Fuck no. "Brother," he says, shaking his head. "Fuck, you have to let her in. Don't you think she deserves to know the truth?"

"No," I say vehemently. "She doesn't. No one needs to know it. Understand?"

"Understood, brother. Trust me, I get it. You don't want to tell her, that's fine, but fuck, it should be told. It'll help her understand a bit more about you and that you're not an asshole for the sake of being one."

I raise a brow. "I'm always an asshole, Wrath. Always have been and always will be."

"You aren't always, Preach, but the shit that you've done is assholeness. Telling Ailbhe what's happened will help repair the relationship. It will make things easier for you."

"That may be so," I growl. "But it ain't fuckin' happenin'."

I can't and won't tell her that. She's got enough shit going on right now. She's stressed, and the last thing she needs is my shit on top of all that. My past is exactly that, my fucking past, and it needs to stay where the fuck it belongs, and that's nowhere near Ailbhe or the baby.

"Whatever helps you sleep at night, brother. Just know that we're behind you. We'll do whatever it takes to help you get through all this."

My chest warms and the pain lifts a bit. "Appreciate that, brother," I say with gratitude. My brothers are my family, and I'll do whatever the hell it takes to ensure they're safe. I have their backs and they have mine.

"There's a party tonight," he says. "Just wanted you to know."

Fuck. That's not what I need right now. I've not touched a drop of alcohol for the past three weeks. I lapsed on the first week after finding out what happend with Ailbhe and Pyro set me straight. I'm trying, I'm truly fucking trying. It's been a fucking month since I fucked up even more with Ailbhe. I'm trying to be responsible. It's fucked up. The dreams are back in full force and I'm barely sleeping. I hate that I'm not able to drown my sorrows, but fuck, I need to get my shit together.

"What time?" I ask, wondering if I should go to the club tonight instead.

"Sorry, brother, but you're here tonight," he says through his laughter. The fucker damn well knows what he's doing.

"Fuck," I groan. This is the last fucking thing I need. "Anyone gets drunk and pisses me off, I'm goin' to end up knockin' them the fuck out."

He gets to his feet, still laughing. "Trust me, brother, we're all well aware of what'll happen if anyone pisses you off."

I know I'm an asshole, that I'm struggling. I'm terse with everyone and I bite everyone's head off.

"Preacher," I hear the sultry tone of Silver. The club whores here are sweet. Then again, the ones back in New York were too at the beginning, and then everything went to shit. I've learned my lesson with this shit and it won't be happening again.

"Silver, now ain't the time," I say through clenched teeth. The woman's gorgeous, but she's not my type.

She pouts as she presses against me. "What's wrong?" she purrs, and I roll my eyes. That shit isn't sexy. "You don't want to have fun?"

"Nope," I hiss.

She doesn't listen. Instead, she moves in front of me and climbs onto my lap.

"Now, this is better," she says, wiggling her ass on my crotch. "Why are you always so angry? I could help ease the tension."

"Not happenin'," I snap.

This bitch is not fucking listening. Christ, she's desperate.

"You're the last brother who's single."

Ah, that's what's up with her. She's wanting a brother. That's not going to fucking happen. Raptor was all about to having fun but that shit stopped when he met Mallory. It's been almost two years since he last saw her and he's still looking for her. She's good at hiding, and she doesn't want to be found. The question is: why? What is she hiding from, Raptor or someone else?

I feel someone's gaze on me, and it's heated. I glance around, trying to figure out who it is, but then I hear Wrath. "Fuck," he growls low. "Ailbhe, it's not what it looks like."

His words hit me, and I turn to where he is and see Ailbhe standing at the door. She's dressed in a tight pair of jeans and a tank top. She's fucking gorgeous, always has been. She looks a lot better than the last time I saw her. She's stronger today, which means she's getting better.

"Ailbhe," I say, wondering what the fuck is going on.

She glares at me, her eyes filled with anger and hatred.

"Who's the bitch?" Silver asks with disgust in her voice.

I push her off my lap and get to my feet. "You're done," I snap. "Get your fuckin' shit and get the fuck out of here." I turn to where Ailbhe's standing and realize that she's gone. Fuck. She's gone.

"What?" Silver shrieks. "You can't do this."

"Yes, he can," Chloe snaps as she steps up to where we are. "You're done here. It's time for you to leave." She turns to me. "You need to sort this out, Preacher. Ailbhe doesn't know this world. She came here for a reason and she's hurt. You need to go and speak with her. I'll deal with Silver."

I don't spare the bitch a second look as I stalk out of the clubhouse. I'm praying Ailbhe is still here. Thankfully, when I walk outside, she's standing by her car, arms crossed over her chest as she talks with Wrath and Hayley. Everyone turns to watch me as I move toward her.

"Easy, Preach," Wrath warns. "You've got to tread carefully now, brother."

I nod. I fucking know that. "I will. Can y'all give me and Ailbhe a moment?"

Hayley nods, her eyes soft as she glances between Ailbhe and I. "Sure. Ailbhe, it was so lovely to meet you. I hope you'll come back again."

"It was good to meet you. Thanks for talking with me."

I already knew that Chloe likes Ailbhe, and now Hayley's making it obvious that she does too. While I'm glad that they do, it just makes things a whole lot harder for me to try and navigate this situation.

"I'm sorry," I say the moment we're alone together. "I swear that nothin' happened between Silver and I. She sure as fuck wanted it to."

"She was on your lap," she replies dryly. "And you're saying nothing happened. Why was she there?"

"I should have pushed her off the moment she got

there. I can assure you that I never fucked her. You're the only one I've been with."

She glances away, her eyes filled with tears. "Okay," she says softly. "I only came here to let you know that I've decided on having a paternity test."

Relief washes through me. Fuck, I thought I'd have to talk to her about it again, but she's here and giving it to me. "Thank you."

She nods. "But we're done," she says harshly. "I don't want to see you or even speak to you. You want this, then you're paying for it. I've got four kids to support. I don't have the money to do this shit."

"Whatever you need," I reply instantly. "How much is it?"

She lifts her shoulders and shrugs. "I don't know. I'm booked in for next week to have it done. I mean what I said, Preacher. I don't want to talk to you and I don't want to see you."

I swallow hard. It fucking sucks hearing her say those words. "You've got it."

She shakes her head. "You really are a fucking dickhead, aren't you?" The look of utter disgust on her face makes me want to fucking hide. She hates me. I can see how badly I've fucked up. "Why can't you fight? I mean, do you actually care about me?"

I don't say anything. If she knew the truth, it would give her false hope. That's something I don't want to give her. I want her. Christ, I've never wanted anyone as much as I want her. But I'm too fucked up for anything other than fucking. I'm so twisted deep inside that I'd hurt her more than if I weren't with her.

The tears fall down her face unchecked, and she shakes her head before turning around and climbing into her car. She doesn't say a word to me as she backs out of the parking lot and drives away.

I can't seem to do anything right when it comes to Ailbhe. I never wanted to hurt her. Fuck, it's the last thing I want, but it's all that I seem to be able to do.

I have no fucking idea what's going to happen now. What if that paternity test comes back positive? What happens then?

Christ, I can't do this. I really can't fucking do this. It feels as though everything that I've done is crumbling down around me. How do I always manage to fuck everything up?

I need help, and there's only one person I know who can help me.

Fuck. It's time to go home and regroup. I need Reaper to help set me straight. He's the only one who truly knows me and he'll give me the kick up the ass that I need. But that means going back and seeing Tyson. Can I manage that?

Fuck.

CHAPTER 19
AILBHE

"You feeling better?" Tamara asks with a smile as she wraps her arms around me.

I'm finally back at work and I'm feeling better. I'm stronger, and I'm able to eat and drink without vomiting it all back up. It's been weeks since I was in hospital, and thankfully, I'm back to normal. The pregnancy is progressing nicely and the baby is growing perfectly. Yesterday, I had the paternity test. It's going to take a few days for the results to come back.

"I'm feeling better," I promise her.

She grins. "Good. It's been lonely around here without you. Kelsie has gone part-time and I only see her a few times a week now."

"Yeah, I haven't seen her in a while. She has texted a few times to check in." It's shit that she's not here full-time, but I'm proud of her. She's doing what she loves. She's worked her arse off and she's achieving her dream.

"So what's happening with you and Preacher? Last I heard he asked for a paternity test."

I groan. I called Tamara the night it happened and unloaded everything on her. She's been there for me throughout everything I'm going through. She's been a rock and I'm lucky to have her. Hell, I'm lucky as hell to have Tamara and my family. They've kept me sane the past few weeks.

"Oh no. What the hell happened?"

I quickly replay everything that's happened, trying my hardest not to cry again. I've done that enough. I've made myself a promise not to shed any more tears over Preacher. The man's caused me enough pain as it is. "I've not heard from him since I left the clubhouse."

She shakes her head. "Damn, what the hell is wrong with him? I mean, it's not as though you've put any pressure on him. You've basically told him you're not wanting anything from him, so why's he acting this way?"

I lean backward. "Ugh, if you find out, can you let me know? I'm sick of trying to work out what's going through his head. It's hard enough to work out my own mind, let alone his."

"For me, I'm focusing on ensuring the baby's okay

and I get through this pregnancy, and that the kids are all okay."

I've decided that I'm only focusing on myself and my family. Preacher's a grown fucking man and he's accountable for his own actions, and I can't change them or make him do anything he doesn't want to do. I'm not going to chase him, nor am I going to be the one to cry and weep and make him feel guilty for whatever the hell he's doing. No. I'm staying strong and focusing on myself, my baby, and my family.

"Look at you," she beams with pride. "I'm so damn proud of you."

I return the smile. It took a while for me to be okay with the decision I've made, but it's the right one to make and I'm at peace with it.

"It's time to get to work," I tell her. "I need to make money. I need to pay Jed, and the prick will no doubt come to the house if I'm not paid in full on Monday morning."

"That bastard needs to go to hell. Your dad's a dick for putting you in that position, Ailbhe. No way in hell my dad would do that to me. I'm pretty sure my mam would kill him if he ever tried."

"Yeah, well my parents aren't exactly the best now, are they? They never were fit enough to become parents, and they only made things worse by popping out more and more children over the years."

"Are you worried about what's going to happen when the baby comes?" she asks as she reaches for my hand. "It's going to be tough. You'll have six children under eighteen living in your house and you'll be working nights. That's rough going."

"With Ruairi helping me pay off Da's debt, we should have it paid off by the time the baby arrives. When the time comes for me to be back to work, I'll be able to afford to pay a babysitter to watch the children while I'm working."

She gifts me a soft, sweet smile. "You've really been thinking hard about this, haven't you?"

I nod. "I have. Ruairi's also let me know that he can help whenever I need it. Which I adore, but I'm not sure if I would feel comfortable putting that much pressure on him."

I love my brother, but he's not at ease around our brother and sisters as it is. I wouldn't want to add another child to the mix to add to that pressure he's feeling. It's not fair, and I would hate if someone did it to me. Paying for a qualified child minder who knows what they're doing isn't going to make me destitute, not after the debt Da's in has been paid off. It would probably be cheaper to pay the child minder a week's wages than to pay his debt.

"Your brother is hot. You really need to introduce him to me."

I roll my eyes. "Girl, you are not going there. You are a queen. I love my brother but you are so much better than that."

She waves me away. "I like them rough, and from everything I've heard, girl, he is rough with a capital R."

I can't contain my laughter. "Girl, really?"

She giggles like a schoolgirl. "Really. So do me a favor and introduce me to him."

"Fine, you've got it. I'll introduce you to him. But I'm warning you. Ruairi is a player and I don't want you to get hurt."

"I won't. I can keep my feelings out of it, babe. So don't worry about me, okay?"

They're both adults and they're able to do whatever they want. I can't control anyone and I shouldn't try to. So if she wants to get to know Ruairi, I'm not going to stop her.

She bounces away from me, smiling and giddy. I love seeing her so happy. This is all I want, for those that I love to be happy.

"Ready?" Tamara asks hours later. I'm dead on my feet and ready to drop. It's been a good day. I've managed to work a full shift and make some good money. I should be able to have the money to pay Jed this week, especially with Ruairi chipping in and helping out.

"I'm ready," I say as I reach for my bag. I'm a little disappointed that Preacher wasn't here. I thought he would be. I really thought that he'd be here. It shows me yet again that I really don't know him. I keep getting my hopes up and they're getting dashed each and every time.

"Forget about him, babe," Tamara whispers. "He's not worth the pain."

He truly isn't worth the bloody pain. It's just hard. Whenever I think there's a glimmer of hope that he'll change or show up, he doesn't and I'm left reeling. I need to stop setting myself up for failure.

"Ailbhe," Wrath greets me as we exit the club. He's around a lot more than he used to be. Since Preacher found out I'm pregnant, he's not been around the club. Instead, either Wrath or Pyro have been here. I know they're watching me, that they're keeping an eye on me.

"Hey," I say as I walk past him toward my car.

"You got a minute?" he asks, and my steps falter.

"I'll talk to you later, okay?" Tamara says as she carries on walking toward her father's car that's parked waiting for her.

"Bye, honey, I'll see you later," I reply and turn back to Wrath. "What's wrong?"

"I wanted to check in on you," he says. "Hayley's been worried about you too."

"I'm doing okay," I assure him. "You and your wife are sweet for asking."

"That's good, sweetheart," he says with a smile.

I have a feeling that he's not only asking for his wife. "Where is he, Wrath?"

He sighs. "He's gone back to New York. He'll be back soon."

I blink, surprised by his answer. "Oh," I say, feeling a little uneasy. "I hadn't realized he was going back."

Did he go to New York because of me? Is he really coming back or is this it?

"He'll be back, Ailbhe. I can promise you that. He'll be back."

I don't believe him. I don't know why, but there's a part of me that thinks he's just saying that Preacher will be home when he's not actually going to.

"Thanks for telling me," I say. "I'll see you later."

He nods. "If you ever need anythin', just let me know."

I flash him another smile. "I appreciate that, Wrath. Thank you."

I turn and walk to my car, my heart racing. I'm sad Preacher's gone. I can't help but feel as though he's gone because of me. Because of the baby. Had I not gotten pregnant, would he have gone back to the States?

God, why is everything so fucked up? I had hoped it would have been plain sailing from here on out, but things never go to plan.

I need to finally realize that my baby only has me. Preacher's never going to come around and be a father. He's run as far as he can, and I don't think he'll ever be back.

CHAPTER 20
PREACHER

I'm a fucking coward. That's exactly what the fuck I am. When the going gets tough, I run.

When Abel committed suicide and died, I ran and never came back. Granted it was going to happen anyway as I was already leaving, but he hung himself, and instead of staying and saying my goodbyes, I left and never looked back. When that shit went down with Reaper going to prison, instead of running somewhere, I found my escape at the bottom of a bottle. Then Tyson happened and I couldn't cope, so I ran, and I also drank as much as I could. Now here I am again, doing everything but facing the challenges ahead of me.

The ride from the airport to the clubhouse is quiet. One of the new prospects have come and collected me. Something I'm extremely grateful for. I didn't want to have the small chit-chat with anyone else. It's fucked up enough that I'm even here. I should be in Ireland sorting my shit out, but instead, I need my brother to kick my ass and help me clear my fucking head.

I called Reaper last night. It was the fourth time in a year that I've spoken to him. That's beyond fucking crazy. The guy has always been at my side and I fucking left and never looked back. Yet again, I called him, telling him that I needed him, and he didn't even hesitate. He told me he'd be waiting for me. That's true brotherhood. Utter loyalty. I don't know what I'd do without him. Even after a year has passed and with an ocean between us, it hasn't changed how he views me. I'm still his brother.

If only I was able to deal with my shit the way he is. Instead, I bottle everything up until I can't handle it any longer and then I need to escape. It's fucking crazy how I handle shit.

The New York scenery hasn't changed. It's just the same as I left. A few more high rises but nothing has drastically changed. "Preacher," the prospect says. "We're arriving now."

I nod my head in thanks. The dude's telling me something I already know.

"Oh, Preach," I hear the soft sound of Esme's voice and my heart races as I glance at her. She's pregnant, noticeably pregnant. She moves toward me, a little hesitant, and I fucking hate that. This woman is my brother's old lady. I'd lay my life down on the line for her. I open my arms and she rushes into them, crashing into me and holding on tight. "It's so good to see you," she tells me. "I'm so glad you're here."

How the fuck do I tell her that I'm not sure how long I'm here for? I shouldn't even have come.

"Is Reaper here?" I ask, my voice terse.

She shakes her head. "He's on his way with Ace. The other guys are here. They're waiting to see you."

My jaw clenches. Fuck, I don't want to see them. I only came to see Reaper, Ace, and Stag. Those men I trust. Those are the ones that I know without a doubt wouldn't judge me for the shit that's gone down. "Don't want to see them right now, Es."

She looks up at me, her cheeks red and her eyes wide. "Oh, um, of course. How about you wait in Ace's office while he and Grayson are on their way?" I nod and she leads the way.

Every step I take is heavy and filled with pain. I shouldn't be here. I knew the moment I made the call to Reap that I shouldn't be coming here. Hell, I almost didn't get on the damn flight.

I sit down in Ace's office and wait for him and Reaper to join me. I'm praying that I've made the right decision in being here and seeking help. It could be the biggest mistake of my life, but I'm hoping that it's not.

Ailbhe is sweet and fucking amazing. I have to have some sort of faith that she'll forgive me, and that when all this shit is said and done, she'll understand that it wasn't about her, but due to my own fucking past.

The door opens and I glance at it. In walks Ace. The man has always had a presence. He's six-one and full of muscles. The man is one of the best men I know, and he's probably the fairest and most loyal man too. My gaze passes him and I see Reaper. Fuck, it hurts to see him. He's not changed much since I left, but the worry in his eyes as he watches me is what fucking guts me. I've been an ass by not talking to him. Behind Ace and Reaper is Stag. The man's bald as the day is long, his beard is trimmed, and he's got a weird smile on his face. I get it, I've changed a fucking lot in the past year. I'm a mess, and I fucking look it too.

I get to my feet and do something I haven't done in a fucking year. I pull Reaper in for a hug. "Fuckin' good to see you, brother," I say, and it's true. It's so fucking good to see him.

"You too, man. What the fuck is goin' on?" he asks as he pats my back. I can tell he's on edge, no doubt ready to step in and do whatever is needed to help me out.

I step backward and sigh, running a hand through my hair. I glance between the three men in front of me. "I fucked up. I'm an asshole. I met a woman, Ailbhe."

Christ, even saying her name has pain spearing through my chest.

Ace takes a breath, no doubt relieved that it's nothing serious. "Okay, sit down and tell me what the fuck happened. Christ, man, you fuckin' scared us. We thought you were on the run like Wrath."

Wrath killed Hayley's foster parents. Those cunts allowed their grown-ass son to groom and rape Hayley when she was a teenager. Hayley became pregnant, and that asshole of a son of theirs died. They turned their focus on Hayley's daughter, Eva, wanting to raise her. Hayley ran, but those fuckers found her and hurt her. Wrath's not a man to let anyone harm his family—none of us are—so he ended the threat once and for all. He's now wanted in connection for their murder, hence why he and his wife and family live in Ireland and not here. The man's happy, as is his family, and as long as he doesn't return to America, he should be good.

"No. Ailbhe is a stripper in the club we own. She's sweet and fuckin' gorgeous. One thing led to another and we ended up fuckin'. " I was an asshole with her. It was all that I could fucking give her and yet I fucked that up too. "As I said, she's sweet and too fuckin' good for me. Well, a few weeks ago, she told me she's pregnant."

Reaper winces. "Fuck. What did you say?" He, above anyone else, knows the depths of how bad it hurt me when the shit went down with Pepper and I found out that Tyson wasn't mine. Reaper knows the pain because he's felt it too.

"I called her a liar and told her to get the fuck away from me." I can't keep the anger and self-loathing out of my voice. "Then a month ago, she collapsed when she was on stage and was rushed to hospital. She's pregnant alright. She's also gettin' sick all the time and isn't gettin' enough water. She's dehydrated."

"So what happened then?" Ace asks. "Did you speak with her?" I've got his full attention. His arms are crossed over his chest as he leans against his desk.

I shake my head. God, I wish it were that damn fucking simple. "No, she told me to fuck off, that she doesn't need me to raise her baby and that I need to go sit on a giant cactus and fuck myself."

Reaper chuckles. No doubt he's loving that Ailbhe's giving me a hard time.

"Okay, so the question is: is the baby yours?" Stag asks. "Did you explain what happened with Tyson, man?"

I sigh. I knew this question was going to be asked. "No, I haven't spoken about Tyson, and Ailbhe was a virgin when I fucked her."

"So talk to her, make her understand that you're an asshole and explain what happened. I'm sure she'll understand," Reaper says.

I wish it were that fucking easy. "She came to see me, and when she did, one of the club whores was sitting on my lap."

"Christ," Ace growls. "Tell me you weren't fuckin' her?"

"No," I snarl, affronted that he'd even think that. Christ, that woman has me tied up in knots. I can't think of anyone but her. "I haven't fucked anyone since I got with Ailbhe."

"So you like her," Reaper says pointedly, and I nod. "Then clean yourself up. You said this girl is sweet and that she was a virgin when you got together. Go fuckin' talk to her, man, explain everythin' you've just said to us and pray that she listens to you."

"From what you've said, this is your child, Preach, but I'd still get a paternity test," Ace cautions me. "If she's as sweet as you say, then she'll understand. But bein' here isn't goin' to help you. In fact, it's goin' to make things harder."

I run a hand over my face. I have no fucking idea what to do. "I've really fucked up with her."

"We've all fucked up somehow," Stag tells him. "Fuck, Kins walked in on me fuckin' a club whore. You got to work at makin' amends."

"Fuck," I snarl. "Fine." They're right, but I have no damn idea how to go about it and that's what I need help with.

"But first, you need to get sober, clean up, and start takin' care of yourself," Reap says, and I know that he's angry, but he's holding it back and trying to help me. "Come on, man, let's get you upstairs so you can start doin' that."

I nod, knowing he's right. Right now, I need to clean up and look a little less disheveled. Reap leads me toward my old room. He opens the door, and I realize it's been redecorated since I left. Fuck, I'm grateful. It looks completely different, and I know that whoever did it was hoping that if I came back, it wouldn't hold as many memories as it did when I was living here.

"Daddy," I hear a little voice call out.

I stop in my tracks at the threshold to the bedroom and turn to see Tyson running toward Reaper. I see it. I finally fucking see it. Christ, I was so blinded before that I didn't notice what was right in front of my eyes. "Fuck, man, he's your double." He's the image of Reaper. It's no wonder Reap knew Tyson was his the moment he laid eyes on the boy.

Reaper chuckles. "Yeah, he's even into bikes. He's goin' to give Esme gray hairs."

"I heard that," she sighs as she walks toward us, a cup in her hands. "Here, Preach, I made you a coffee. It may help."

Fuck, they're so domesticated. Tyson is right where

he belongs with the two of them. There's no doubting that. But it doesn't stop the jealousy flowing through my veins. He was my boy, my son. I loved him as such, and for a time, I was all that he knew, and now he doesn't even know me.

I give Esme a wink, trying to play off the hurt and jealousy. "Thanks, Es. Still as gorgeous as ever."

"Brother," Reaper warns me. He's very territorial when it comes to his old lady. "I will gut you where you stand. Take your eyes off her."

I can't help but chuckle. It's so easy to rile Reaper up. "Thanks for the coffee, Es. I'm goin' to shower and get some sleep."

Her eyes widen. "So soon? You've just got here."

"It's been a fuckin' long day, Es. I'll see you in the mornin'." I close the door behind me, shutting out the image of the little boy who's now in Reaper's arms. The boy that was once mine.

Christ, maybe coming here wasn't the best idea. The pain that had been numbed is back in full force. Seeing Tyson again, and him not knowing who I am, is fucking gutting. I didn't expect it to hurt. Hell, I didn't expect him to not know who I was.

That's how fucked up I am. I'm so far up my own ass, I can't even see reality.

Damn it. How the fuck am I supposed to find a way out of all this mess without fucking it all up further?

CHAPTER 21
PREACHER

"You still look like shit, brother," Reaper says as he enters my room. He's holding two mugs in his hand and his expression is closed. I have a feeling this is going to be a fucking long and uncomfortable conversation, but it's been a long fucking time coming. "Wanted to let you rest as I knew you'd not been sleepin'. Honestly, Preach, you look like hell."

I chuckle. I can always trust Reaper to lay it on me straight. "I fuckin' feel like hell."

He hands me one of the mugs. "Here drink that. I'm not sure if they have the good stuff over in Ireland."

I take the mug and take a sip of the coffee and wait. He's here for a reason. I'm just going to wait him out. I keep my gaze firmly on him and it doesn't take long for him to get to the point.

"You're a fuckin' asshole, you know that?"

"Yeah, brother, I know. I've fucked up more times than I can count. But I did what was best for me and I did what was best for Tyson. Had I stayed, you and Esme wouldn't have been able to have the connection that you do now." I heard them last night. They're a real family. Had I stayed, that bond they have now would never have been able to happen. I don't think I'd have had the strength to allow it to.

He sighs and glances away. He knows I'm right. "That bein' said, what the fuck is wrong with you? Hmm? You don't answer the millions of calls and texts? You're an asshole, Preacher, a fuckin' asshole."

"I know," I say. "Trust me, brother, I know. But I needed to put space between me and this entire situation. You have no fuckin' idea how it feels to lose a child."

"You didn't have to," he snarls. "I was never goin' to fuckin' take him from you. Not fuckin' ever."

"You say that now, brother, but you didn't know what the future held. You had no idea what would happen a year or two down the line. I made the choice to leave for all our sakes."

"You're a damn martyr," he spits. "I get that you had to go. Fuck, I would have probably done the exact same thing, but, brother, the shit you and I have gone through... Ignorin' me was never the way to go. Not fuckin' ever."

I take a deep breath. This is what he wanted to talk about. Not Tyson. This. "No, it wasn't. But I couldn't listen to you talk about Ty, Reaper. I couldn't bear to listen to how you were playing happy families with him while I was dying with the grief of losing him."

I watch as he swallows hard. "Fuck, brother."

"So while I get that you're pissed, that I fuckin' hurt you, I did what I needed to keep my sanity. I did what I had to in order to keep my sanity."

He flicks his tongue against the piercing on his lip. It's something he does when he's thinking a lot. "Fuck, brother, I hadn't realized it was so bad. Pyro, Raptor, and Wrath didn't say it had gotten that bad."

"Why would they? You know me, Reap. I'm not one to let anyone know how I'm feelin'. Fuck, most of the time, I'm drunk as a fuckin' skunk."

He shakes his head. "Thought you stopped that shit?" he growls.

When he came out of prison, I was in a bad place. I think I'd been drunk the majority of the time he was inside. Thankfully, I was able to pull myself out of the darkness with his and the rest of the brothers' help. I haven't sunk to that depth again. I think mainly because I had Ailbhe to take my mind off things during the nights.

"What happens now? Are you going back to Ireland?" he asks.

My brows knit together at his question. The fuck? Why the hell would he ask me that? "Of course."

He nods. "I had to ask. I wanted to know if I needed to kick your ass to get you back on the plane. But it's good to know you know where you need to be."

"Ailbhe's havin' a baby," I tell him. There's no fucking way I'd be anywhere but where she is.

"You need to help me understand this shit, brother. You want a paternity test, but by the way you're talkin', it's as though you know the baby is yours."

I chuckle. "Yeah, that's about how fucked up my head is. I'm pretty sure Ailbhe's havin' my baby, but I've been burned before. That shit was fucked up, brother. I can't go through that again. No fuckin' way. So I need that test."

He sighs. "I get where you're comin' from, but you have to understand that askin' the woman for the test tells her that you don't trust her."

I run a hand over my face. "I know," I say through clenched teeth. "I saw the devastation on her face when I asked for it."

He winces. "That went down well, I take it?"

I glare at him. "About as well as a fuckin' snake bite. Now she wants nothin' to do with me. Hence why I need your help. You're the only one who knows me. Tell me how the fuck I make things right?"

He gives me a look, one that has me biting back a curse. "You already know the answer to that."

I shake my head. "Not openin' up those wounds, brother. I'll do anythin' but that."

"There's no other way, Preach. There truly isn't. You need to tell her the truth and believe that she'll be understandin'. Everythin' you've said about her so far tells me that she'll be more than understandin'."

Of that I have no fucking doubt, but having to open up my old wounds and let it all out... That's not something I ever do. Not fucking ever. Reaper knows about the shit that went down with my parents and Abel because I was drunk one night. It was the fifth anniversary of Abel's death, and I was a fucking drunken mess and let it slip what was up. He never repeated it to anyone, just as I haven't repeated his past to anyone. It's why we're so close. We have trust in one another.

"You're goin' to have to go back and grovel."

I look at him with wide eyes. "The fuck is that?"

He chuckles. "Apologize and beg for her forgiveness. Get down on your knees and pray to every god there is that she'll forgive you, brother."

I narrow my eyes. "You're lovin' this a little too fuckin' much."

He shrugs. "Gotta get my entertainment from somewhere."

Ass. "So you're sayin' that the only way for me to make her forgive me is by being truthful and openin' up about the past?"

"Unfortunately, brother, that's exactly what you're goin' to have to do."

I grit my teeth. Fuck. That's the last damn thing I want to do.

My bedroom door opens and Ace storms in, his eyes filled with anger and his jaw clenched. "Brother, I have to tell you somethin' and I need you to stay calm."

"The fuck is goin' on?" Reaper asks.

My stomach fucking drops. "Ailbhe?" I ask, knowing that it has to do with her. There's no one else he'd tell me to be calm about. Reaper's right in fucking front of me.

"I got a call from Py. He's caught me up to speed with Jed O'Connor and the shit he's been doin'," Ace says, and I take a steadying breath. Fuck, he really needs to be careful with his words. I thought Ailbhe was in trouble. Christ, my heart is fucking pounding.

Reaper glances between the two of us. "Someone wanna catch me up?"

"Jed is a loan shark. From everythin' Denis and his boys have said, Jed gives money out like it's free. He knows they'll not be able to repay it so he takes the debt from others instead," I tell him. "He has them repay him in other ways."

Reaper's lip curls into a snarl. "Christ, what a fuckin' bastard."

"We heard him talk to one guy who'd passed his debt off onto his daughter and Jed wanted her. Stephen Maguire had his friend try to figure out who it was. We haven't heard anythin' since then."

Ace's jaw clenches. "Py got a visit from Freddie Kinnock and Stephen Maguire. Turns out, Freddie knows the girl's brother. He and Stephen were good friends with the guy."

"Prez, man," Reap says low. "Whatever the fuck you're tryin' to say, will you spit it the fuck out?"

"Their friend is a guy called Ruairi Mangan."

My heart stops and I stare at Ace. "Tell me you're fuckin' lyin'."

"Wouldn't do that to you, brother. You know I wouldn't. Pyro wants me to let you know that he and Wrath are goin' to her house and bringin' her and the kids to the clubhouse. They want them safe. He wanted me to tell you that."

My chest is burning with rage. I shouldn't have left. I should have stayed in Dublin. Had I have done, then I would be with her. I'd be making sure she's okay. Instead, I let my fears get the best of me and ran. Fuck.

"I need to get a flight," I say through gritted teeth.

"Eda's already on it. She's on to Makenna to see if she'll let you use her plane."

I take a deep breath. "Is Ailbhe okay?" I ask, needing him to reassure me that she is. I need him to tell me that my woman is fine.

"Py said he'll call me once he's at her house. Once he calls, I'll let you know."

"Tobias?" Eda calls out in her raspy voice. It's not as noticeable as it was when she first came to the clubhouse. It's fucked up how she came about having her voice. Her mom tried to kill her and would have if her father hadn't stepped in, but her father was a sonofabitch who was worse than her mom.

"In here, babe. You speak with Makenna?"

"Yeah, Kenna said the plane will be ready to go in an hour. She did ask to know who'd be boarding the plane."

"Preacher and I," Ace says. "My brother's girl's in trouble, so I'm goin'. I need you to stay here though, babe."

Eda nods as she slides into Ace's embrace. She flashes me a smile. "Of course."

"I'm comin' too," Reaper says, his voice filled with anger. "Ain't no fuckin' way I'm stayin' behind, and I'm pretty sure Esme would have my balls if I even thought about it."

"You got that, babe?" Ace asks her.

"On it. I'll let Kenna know. Make sure you're all ready to leave within the next ten minutes." Eda's perfect for Ace, and she's really grown into herself. She's no longer afraid of what could happen. She's free to be herself here and every brother loves her.

Ace's cell rings and Reaper moves toward me. I know my brother. He's getting close in case he needs to lock me down. But if something's happened to Ailbhe, I ain't bein' locked down. I'll lose my damn mind.

"Brother," Ace answers. I can't hear what Pyro's saying, but whatever it is, it isn't good. Ace's body is locked tight and he won't look at me. Fuck.

"Preach," he says once he ends the call. "We need to get that flight."

"What we need is for you to tell me what Pyro said. What the fuck happened?"

He shakes his head. "Sorry, brother, but Ailbhe's in the hospital. Jed got to her last night."

My blood runs cold and rage fills my head. Fuck.

I'm going to enjoy killing that cunt. I'm going to strip his skin from him piece by piece.

My heart fucking sinks. Ailbhe... Christ, what the fuck have I done? I shouldn't have left her. I should have stayed in Dublin and kept an eye on her. I should have been with her.

I close my eyes, and for the first time since I was a

boy, I say a silent prayer, pleading with God to make sure she and our baby are safe.

CHAPTER 22
AILBHE

'm trying to rush the kids out of the door. They're going to be late if they don't get a wriggle on. Today, I overslept, which means everyone has. Now, I have more energy and I'm eating and drinking —more than normal. But I'm so damn exhausted when my head hits the pillow, I'm sleeping like the dead.

"Ailbhe," Mikey says as he walks into the kitchen. "Seriously, we're going to be late. Where the hell is Ruairi?"

I smile. Ruairi and Tamara had a date last night. The last I heard from my girl was that it was going great, and Ruairi didn't come home last night. The plan for him to get his own apartment went down the drain when he found out I was pregnant. He's staying here for a little while longer to help with the bills and to ensure that I'm okay. I think I scared him with how sick I was.

"I know, but better late than never. I would drive you, but the traffic is horrendous so you'll be quicker walking."

He sighs, knowing I'm right. "Fine, but Fiona can walk herself to school. I'll take Evie and Hannah to school and then go myself."

"Hey," Fiona cries. "Why do I have to walk to school alone? Have you seen all the weirdos out there?"

Mikey shakes his head. "Fine, whatever, but get your bag. We're leaving now."

I smile. As much as they all annoy one another, they're all very protective. He wouldn't let Fiona go alone, not when she's worried.

"Got it," she shouts as she grabs it from the floor. "Love you, Al," she yells as she runs to the door. "Have a good day."

I laugh. "You too. Be good and I'll see you tonight."

Evie runs over to me and I pull her into my arms. "Have a good day, honey. I'll pick you up after school and you can tell me all about your day."

She gives me a big grin. "Okay, bye, Ailbhe."

Once the kids are gone, I finish cleaning up from breakfast and make sure I have everything I need for dinner. There's nothing worse than coming home after school's finished and realizing there's nothing to cook for the kids. Thankfully, Ruairi did the shopping yesterday and stocked up on everything.

I switch the music on and begin to vacuum. Weekday mornings are the worst, but I try to keep on top of everything that needs to be done. I know that if I don't, it will build up, and I can't live like that.

I'm dancing as I clean, in a world of my own. Two nights ago, I was upset. Finding out that Preacher had left was like a knife to my heart. To my surprise, Tamara was waiting outside my house when I got home. She was worried about me and had her da drop her off. Of course, when I entered the house, both Tamara and Ruairi got on like a house on fire and he took her on a date last night. I'm happy for her, and I'm praying that he behaves himself. I know what Ruairi can be like and I don't want my friend to be upset.

The sound of the front door busting open has me screaming out in fear. My heart races and my blood pumps harder as it rushes to my head. I turn to see Jed standing in the doorway with his three henchmen at his side.

"What the hell?" I cry as I switch the vacuum off. "You can't just break down my door and barge into my home."

Jed stalks toward me, but I hold my ground, hoping I'm not showing fear. That man terrifies me and I hate how damn sleazy he is. He gives me the heebie-jeebies.

I'd do anything to ensure I'm nowhere near him. It's why I have Ruairi pay the debt to Tony. I'd rather not be around any of them.

"My money," Jed sneers. "I warned you, Ailbhe. I warned you what would happen if you didn't have my money."

"Ruairi met with Tony yesterday," I tell him, my pulse skyrocketing. I'm scared, so fucking scared. What's Jed going to do?

"Well, he didn't, and we've not heard from him today. You were warned that you'd be liable for any missed payments, Ailbhe, and would you look, there's a missed payment yesterday."

I shake my head. "No," I say, my mouth feeling dry. "There's no way. We always pay. We do. Let me call Ruairi and see where he is."

I can't believe my brother. What the hell is he thinking? He has one job to do on a Monday morning. If he couldn't do it, he should have told me. I would have met with Tony and paid the damn thing.

"Do you have the money for me, Ailbhe?" he snarls.

I shake my head. I don't. I only have a couple of hundred in the house, and that's nowhere near what Jed wants. "I don't. Are you sure Tony's telling the truth?"

His grin is anything but friendly. "Thing is, Ailbhe, when I found out that Tony was skimming from me, lying to me about payments, I got rid of him."

I swallow hard. Does he mean got rid of him by firing him or got rid of him by killing him?

"So it's been me who has been meeting with Ruairi every Monday morning. Let me tell you that I was displeased to be left waiting with nothing."

Oh God, Ruairi, what have you done?

"Please," I plead with him, bile rising up my throat. "Give me until tomorrow and I'll have your money for you."

He shakes his head. "I want my money now, Ailbhe, right fucking now. No more games."

Tears well in my eyes. "I don't have it," I whisper, hating that I'm being put in this spot.

The smirk on his face is scary. I take a step backward but there's no point. Jed reaches for me, his hand curling into my hair, tugging it hard.

I cry out, my hands reaching up and clawing against his hand, trying to get him off me. It's no use. God, he's too strong.

"You're fucking sexy, Ailbhe, I'll give you that, but you're a damn stuck up bitch. You should have known that you'd never be free of me. I'll keep letting your da add more money to the debt. I'll make sure you're destitute and begging for more."

"Please," I cry. "Let go of me."

"Not going to happen," he snarls, pulling me toward him. "You think you're better than me, bitch?"

I know I am. I'm not an arsehole who hurts people. I don't tell him that. I have some self preservation.

"This is your last warning, Ailbhe. Next time you miss a payment, I'm going to fuck you."

I'm unable to keep the bile down any longer. My stomach protests and I retch. I try to swallow it down but can't. I vomit all over Jed's shoes.

"Cunt," he snarls as he releases my hair and steps backwards. He glares down at his shoes, and I place a hand against my stomach as it once again feels as though I'm going to throw up.

I'm so focused on not trying to be sick that I'm no longer paying attention to the psychopath in the room. A vicious backhand strikes against my cheek. The force of it rocks my entire body, and I'm unable to stay on my feet. I'm thrown to the floor with the sheer power behind the blow, landing heavily as I do. A pained cry escapes my lips.

"Fucking bitch," Jed sneers as he reaches for me. His hands once again tangle in my hair. He drags me up from the ground by my hair, and the tears fall thick and fast. I can't control them. I'm in too much pain. "You have two days, Ailbhe, two fucking days and I want my money. Double the normal repayments. You're in debt to me. You don't fuck me around."

He keeps one hand tight in my hair. The other, he balls into a fist and pulls it back, before following through. This time, I'm aware of what's happening. I can see it. I know he's going to punch me. I try to dodge it, but he's got such a tight grip on my hair that it's impossible to move.

The blow is hard and heavy. It's painful as it connects with my temple. Spots fill my vision as it blurs, the darkness seeping in. My body feels weightless as Jed releases my hair. I have no energy or power to stop myself from falling back to the ground.

I pass out before I even touch the floor. My last conscious thought is of my baby and that I hope Jed leaves. I couldn't bear to wake up with him having touched me. I don't think I'd survive that.

"Ailbhe." I hear the sound of Ruairi's voice. "Ailbhe, honey, you have to open your eyes. Let me know you're okay. Please, Al, please open them and look at me."

I release a pained cry as I try to open them. God, my head hurts so fucking badly. "Ruairi," I groan.

"Oh God, fuck," he says, his words sounding tortured.

I feel him pull me into his arms. "Talk to me, Al," he breathes. "What's going on? Where are you hurt?"

"Head," I whisper. "It's so sore."

"Anywhere else?" he asks. "The ambulance is on its way. I'm so sorry, I should have been here."

"Jed," I tell him as I try to open my eyes, but wince as the light hits them. I close them again. "He was here."

"I know," he tells me as he runs his hand through my hair. "I know. I saw him and his men driving down the street. I knew they'd been here."

I swallow, trying to push back the groan of pain. "I didn't open the door."

He releases a strangled laugh. "I know," he says. "I know. I'm so sorry."

"You didn't pay yesterday," I whisper. "What happened?"

He's quiet, and I hate that he's not talking. I hate that I'm in so much pain that it hurts to speak, let alone move.

The sound of sirens lets me know the ambulance is here. "I'll make this right," he promises me.

"Freddie," I whisper. "Talk with Freddie."

The pain rises once again and I cry out. The darkness starts to pull me under, and I welcome it. I can't cope with how painful my head is. What the hell did Jed do to me?

CHAPTER 23
PREACHER

"*She's out of hospital and is at the clubhouse.*"

Those words have been going around and around my head for the past two hours. I'm glad she's out, but fuck, I don't think she should be. She's had a really bad case of concussion and she's in a lot of pain. Being out of the hospital isn't the best place for her, not if she's still in pain.

My legs have been jumping the entire flight. I'm antsy, and I can't wait for this plane to touch down. I need to be with Ailbhe. I have no doubt that she'll still be pissed, that she'll scream and tell me to fuck off, but I'm not doing it. I'm not fucking leaving. We've got a lot to talk about.

Finding out that she was hurt and in the hospital again, something snapped inside of my brain. I've known since the moment I saw her that she was different. I knew there was something about her that I craved. That hasn't changed. It never faded. In fact, it's only intensified. I kept my distance to protect her and look how fucking well that turned out.

Going to New York was great as I spoke to Reaper and saw Tyson again. Seeing and hearing how happy he is settled something inside of me. I don't feel as worried as I had once been. I had every faith in Reaper and Esme and their roles as Tyson's parents, but it was my boy I was worried about. But he's doing okay. He's happy and thriving. I feel better about my decision to leave. He's got his parents and that's all I wanted.

"She's goin' to be okay, brother," Reaper says. He's sat beside me the entire flight and hasn't spoken to me until now. He knows me. He knows that I wouldn't have been in the mindset to speak. "She's with our brothers. She's safe."

"I'm goin' to fuckin' kill him," I say thickly, my throat clogged with emotion. The sooner I see Ailbhe and know that she's okay, and I see it with my own two eyes, I'll be better. I'm going to find Jed O'Connor and I'm going to gut the bastard. I'll enjoy every fucking second of it.

"I'll have your back every step of the way. I know how you feel, brother. Trust me, I know. The cunt that took Es..." He shakes his head. "I killed that motherfucker. I watched the asshole who hurt her, burn. I know how you're feelin'. You'll get the revenge you seek. We'll make sure of it."

"What if she lost the baby?" I ask, my words low. It's been on my mind. It's been running through my brain since the moment Ace told me she'd been hurt. If she's lost the baby, I'll fucking lose my shit. There's no doubt about it, I'll go fucking feral.

"Don't borrow trouble, brother," he replies. "Py would have told us had that been the case."

I pray that he's right. I really fucking do. If she's lost our baby, I'll never forgive myself.

The plane touches down thirty minutes later. I'm like a child that's full of energy. I feel caged in and I need to escape. The moment the doors to the plane open, I'm out of my seat and walking toward the plane door, Reaper right behind me, having grabbed my bag from the hold above our heads.

"Preach," Pyro greets me. "You doin' okay?"

I stare my brother in the eyes. He doesn't flinch, but his eyes darken. "What do you think, brother?"

"Yeah, I'd feel the exact same if things were reversed. She's at the clubhouse, and she's safe. She's got a nasty bruise or two on her face, but she's upbeat, though I think that's mainly for the children's sake."

I nod, grateful for the information. "She know I'm comin'?"

He grins. "She does. I can't say she was too pleased

about it, nor was she pleased about comin' to stay with us, but she couldn't argue that it was the safest place for her and the family."

"Thank you."

He nods. "Don't thank me, Preach. This is what we do."

He's right, this is what we do. We're a brotherhood. We take care of one another and our families. My family is his and vice versa. I'd lay down my life for any one of my brothers' families and they'd return the favor.

"Let's get goin'," I say. The urge to see Ailbhe is beating at me. I need to check in on her myself.

It takes almost an hour to get to the clubhouse. Pyro, Ace, and Reaper speak the entire way, catching up. It's been a while since we've all seen one another. Things have been crazy in Dublin since I've arrived. Between businesses and babies, it's been crazy busy, and no one has had a chance to return to New York until me. That was because I ran like a coward. I needed to get my head on my shoulders and see straight. And, boy, have I got my head screwed on. I know what I want and what I need to do. It's not going to be easy, but it'll be worth it.

Ailbhe's worth it.

"Oh, Jaysus," I hear the low rumble of Mikey as I

step into the clubhouse. "I was wondering when you'd be back."

I grin at the kid. He's protective of his sister, something that I respect and admire. "It's good to see you too, kid," I say as I move past him in search of his sister.

"She's upstairs in the room, which she said was yours," Mikey shouts at me as I edge toward the stairs.

I turn and grin at Chloe, who's sitting beside Mikey with a smile on her face. Oh, she knows exactly what she's doing. I need to thank her later.

I take the stairs two at a time, and when I reach the top, I see the door to my room is slightly ajar, and I'm wondering if she has it open for a reason.

Entering the room, it takes everything in me not to lose my shit. She's lying on the bed, her eyes closed. I'm glad she's resting, but her beautiful pale skin is marred with two dark, ugly bruises. One on her cheek and the other on her head that covers her eye. That cunt hit her hard and left bruises. I'm definitely going to enjoy killing the fucking cunt.

"Hey," I say softly, not wanting to upset her. I feel awkward, unsure of what to say, but I'm not leaving.

She opens her eyes and gingerly sits up. "Hi," she replies. "I wasn't sure if you were coming home."

Christ, she really has a low opinion of me, not that I

can blame her. I haven't given her any reason to think differently.

"I was always comin' back, Ailbhe. Always."

She nods, but her eyes are void of emotion. She doesn't believe me.

"Are you busy?" I ask. "I want to talk to you about why I'm such an asshole."

Her lips twitch, and I feel as though that's a great start. "Of course not. Take a seat, Preacher. You're making me nervous standing up."

I sink down onto the bed and face her. "I was born to parents who were cunts," I say, unable to keep the snarl from my voice. "They were violent. My father was a pastor, and he used the Bible to teach lessons. If he deemed me to do something wrong, he'd punish me while reciting passages from the Bible." I run a hand through my hair in agitation. I fucking hate talking about this shit. "They're people that I haven't seen since I turned eighteen. I'll never fucking see them again either."

"Oh, Preacher, I'm so very sorry."

"Nothin' for you to apologize for, babe. It was a long time ago." I take a steadying breath and glance away. Fuck, this is going to be hard. "My brother was younger than me. He too felt the wrath of our parents. It was brutal, Ailbhe, so fucking brutal. I told him I was leaving, and the morning I was due to go, he hanged himself."

I hear her gasp and turn to her. I see tears falling from her eyes and hate that she's upset. I fucking hate seeing them fall. "Oh, Preacher," she whispers. "God, I'm so sorry."

I nod. "He was a good kid. He was so fuckin' funny, and he was full of life, but they beat him down. Christ, they beat us both until we were shells of who we were." I grind my jaw. This is a lot fucking harder than I thought it would be. "I despise everything to do with religion."

Her eyes narrow and darken as she curls her lip into a snarl. "Why did you get the name Preacher then?"

I chuckle. "It's my road name that was given to me by my brothers. It's ironic. Same as Bozo's is."

She shakes her head. "You had a traumatic childhood. They shouldn't have given you that name."

I fucking love that she's angry for me. But she shouldn't be. "Trust me, babe, if I had a problem with it, I'd have said so."

She swipes away her tears. "I just hate that you've been through so much. God, I love my siblings. I love them so very much, I couldn't imagine losing them. I'm so sorry for your loss."

"It happened a long time ago now, Ailbhe."

"It doesn't matter how long ago it happened. It still happened, and you lost someone you loved dearly."

"I went through a lot of dark places. I found a home with the Fury Vipers, a brotherhood. I was lucky."

She grins. "They seem amazing, and they've all had great things to say about you. I'm glad you found your home."

"I almost lost it," I tell her, knowing that I need to get it all out. If I don't, I'll lose my nerve and probably won't bring it up again.

"What do you mean?" she asks, her brows furrowed. She's cute when she's confused. Her nose scrunches up and her freckles seem to draw closer together.

"I was out one night and this guy was being a dick, kept coming at us. You know the type, big mouth, full of shit, and looking for a fight."

She grins. "Have you met my brother Ruairi yet?"

I chuckle. "Well, this fucker was dying for a fight and he got it." I shake my head. "I'm a good fighter, babe. I beat that fucker until he was moving no longer."

Her lips form an 'O'. "Did you get into trouble?"

I shake my head. "Almost did, but thankfully, I was able to get on with my life. He, however, never recovered from the injuries I gave him."

"Did you set out that night to hurt him?"

"Fuck no. Hell, I didn't want to fight. But, babe,

there's only so much you can push a man before he snaps, and he pushed me too fuckin' far."

"What else happened? I have a feeling you've got a lot more to tell me," she says softly. The back off stance has gone, thankfully, and she's engaging with me. She's not so standoff-ish any longer.

"A few years back, that asshole's brother met us in a club. He wanted revenge, so he baited me into a fight, and Christ, I gave into him and did it. I beat him just as I did his brother. I swear to you, babe, I don't have an anger problem." I need her to realize that it's not a common occurrence.

She nods. I see that she believes me and I'm glad of it. If she didn't, I'm not sure where we'd go from here.

"That fucker set me up. He called the cops, and when Reaper, my brother, came out of the club, the sirens sounded. Reaper did something that I'll never be able to repay. He took the fall and said he was the one who had the fight with the ass."

"Oh wow," she cries, her tears falling once again.

"He served four years in prison for me, Ailbhe. Had it been me who pleaded guilty, I would have been serving hard time."

"He's a good friend, Preacher. The man loves you."

I close my eyes. God... "You've no idea just how much." I inhale deeply. "I was buried in guilt. My best friend went to prison for me. So I drank myself into a stupor. I found my solace at the bottom of a bottle. I couldn't function with the guilt that I had. When Reaper was released, he set me straight. I was able to work through it all. He was out and he was home. I wasn't feeling as bad as I had when he was inside."

"I bet. That's a lot of guilt to carry. I'm not sure I'd have been able to handle it."

"Did you meet the club whores?" I ask, and her brows narrow once again, but she nods. "In New York, there was a woman named Pepper. She was someone everyone got along with. She never got attached and was a great time." I sigh when I see the hurt slash through her eyes. I get it. Had she spoken about another guy, I'd be pissed. "Pepper got pregnant, and she was five months along before she told anyone. She was playing the brothers, not letting anyone know who the father was. It was fucked up."

"You?" she asks softly.

I nod. "She told me I was the dad. Pepper wasn't as stable as we thought. She was doin' drugs, drinkin', and fuckin' anyone who walked. She was a cunt. Even the day she gave birth to Tyson she was off her face on drugs, babe. She was high as a fuckin' kite as she was deliverin' my son."

"What?" she hisses. "Oh fuck. Where's your boy now?"

I don't answer the question. Not yet anyway. "Tyson

was born addicted to drugs. He spent the first weeks of his life in the hospital. He was a fighter."

She grins. "Hence the name."

"Hence the name. He's a fighter and he deserved the name of one. I killed Pepper, Ailbhe. I killed her with my bare hands. That's the man that I am. I don't make excuses for who I am and I won't apologize for it."

"I'm not stupid, Preacher. I've always known there is a darkness within you."

"One day, when Tyson was a couple months old, one of my brother's told me that Tyson wasn't mine. That he couldn't be due to our blood types."

"No," she whispers. "Oh God, Preacher, please no. Tell me he was lying?"

"He wasn't," I say through a lump in my throat. "He was tellin' the truth. Tyson isn't my son. In fact, he's Reaper's."

She closes her eyes, and her chest heaves as the tears fall. "Oh God."

"I had planned on running, taking my boy and running. Then I found out that Reaper was his father and I couldn't do that to him." I swallow back the tears. Fuck, talking about this is fucking hard. "Reaper had known that Tyson was his, and he was willing to let me continue to raise him."

"You have the best fucking friends."

I chuckle. "I do. But I couldn't keep his son from him, so I left and ended up here. I went back so that Reaper could kick my ass and help me get my head on straight. I'm so fucked up from the past that I kept hurting you with what I was saying."

She's silent for a moment. "I get why you're the way you are. It doesn't excuse the way you've treated me, but I understand it. I'm pregnant with your child, Preacher, and the test results are due any day now. I'm not angry anymore that you asked. In fact, I'm glad we're getting them done so there's no question. I'm an emotional wreck, and I was hurt thinking you didn't trust me."

Relief washes through me. The baby's okay. Thank fucking God.

"I do," I tell her emphatically. "I'm just fucked up."

She nods. "If you want to be a part of our child's life, then no more drinking." She holds up her hand to stop me from speaking when I open my mouth. "You do drink a lot. You've told me as much. I want my baby to have a dad who's happy and alive. So please, think about it."

I respect that she wants me to be happy and healthy. "I've had one bad night in the past three weeks. I'm trying."

"I'm glad that you are," she says through a yawn. "I'm so damn tired."

"The baby is taking your energy. Go to sleep, babe. We'll talk again soon."

"Thank you for coming back."

I get to my feet, relieved that she listened, though I'm not surprised that she was so understanding. "I wasn't planning on staying away. You've gotten me hooked, babe. I can't stay away from you. I've never been able to."

"You're a funny man, Preacher, but I'm glad you're here." She lies down and snuggles into the pillow. "I wish I knew what your name is. I don't want to call you Preacher any longer."

I lean down and press a kiss to her head. "My name's Kane, babe."

She moans in the back of her throat. "Kane. I love it," she slurs. "Night, Kane."

I smile. Maybe, just maybe, things are looking up. "Night, babe. Sleep well. We've got the kids. They're safe here."

I close the door behind me, relieved that she's here and she's safe. Now that I have her here, I'm not letting her go. Not fucking ever.

CHAPTER 24
AILBHE

"Morning," I greet everyone as I enter the kitchen. I'm shocked by how many people are actually here. Not only are all the men here, but so are their women. There are two other children in the club, and both belong to Wrath and his wife, Hayley. Their kids are Eva and James. Then there's Chloe Gallagher. She's Pyro's old lady. He's the president of the chapter and has taken great care of me. But I'm shocked to see Chloe's ma here. I know Callie Gallagher. Her daughter Fiadh is Evie's best friend and the two of them have had play dates before.

"Morning, Ailbhe, did you sleep well?" Callie asks.

I nod. "I did." I glance around the room and see that Evie is sitting at the table having breakfast, Fiadh on her right and Hannah on her left. Mikey and Fiona are sitting up at the bar that goes along the back wall. Both have their heads in their phones, no doubt watching some video on social media or texting their friends.

"I'm sorry they were awake so early," Hayley says with a wince. "James woke up crying and in turn woke the entire house."

"Shit, I'm sorry. You've got enough to deal with," I say, feeling awful that they've had to deal with my kids too.

"Wasn't us," Callie says with a grin. "You have Preacher to thank for the kids being up, dressed, and fed. He's been worried about you. As have I. Why didn't you tell me Jed was being a dickhead?"

"Ooh," Evie says with a wide smile. "Ailbhe, Callie said a bad word."

I shake my head at my feisty little six-year-old. "No money, Evie, honey. That only works on your brothers."

What does she do? Stands up and puts her hands on her hips, reminding me so very much of myself as a teenager. "And you. You told me if anyone swears when I'm around, that they have to pay up."

Callie laughs as she reaches into her bag for her purse. "What's the fee?"

"I don't take coins," Evie says instantly, and I bury my head in my hands. Mikey... I'm going to kill him for teaching her that.

"Kid, you drive a hard bargain. But you're right, I said a bad word and I shouldn't have." Callie hands Evie a five euro note, all the while smiling. "I'm surprised Fiadh hasn't started with that. She'd make a fortune in our house."

I shake my head. "Trust me, Evie's more than making a fortune. I had to put money into a bank account as she had saved so much up from catching Ruairi and Mikey swearing."

"Now now, Ailbhe," Fi taunts. "We all know you're one of the worst."

"That may be so," I say with a smile. "But I don't get caught by Evie." I've learned my lesson. That girl may look sweet as pie, but she's quick as hell to demand money if someone says a bad world. I must have given her fifty euro in the span of four days. After that, I was careful about what I said around her. Ruairi and Mikey don't seem to care. They're not curtailing their curses and will just pay up.

"So," Callie says, pulling the conversation back to her. "Why didn't you tell me about Jed? You know who my family is, Al. You know we'd have been able to help."

I sigh as I take a seat down beside her. I feel the heat of a stare on my back, but I don't need to turn to know Kane's here. "I know, and I love that you wanted to help, but honestly, he hadn't bothered me at all. I was paying the debt, and then he called to the house a while back, claiming I hadn't paid, when I had. Tony hadn't given him the money."

Callie pulls in a sharp breath. "Oh, that little shi—" she pauses, catching herself before she says it. "How many people have they done that to?"

"I know. Thankfully, Ruairi came home and got them to leave. Jed said that he got rid of Tony. I really didn't want him to clarify what he meant."

Callie reaches for my hand and holds it tight. "Why the hell are you paying for your da's debt, hon?"

"I didn't have a choice. When Ma left, Da told Jed I'd take care of his debt, and Jed doesn't care. He'll take money from whoever he can get it from." I sigh. "But I was paying it. I needed to do so because I wanted Jed away from the girls."

"I don't blame you," Chloe hisses. "That man is vile. I've heard the stories. He really doesn't discriminate on age, does he?"

I shake my head. "Not from what I've heard." I run a shaky hand through my hair, wincing as my hand brushes against the bruise on my temple. "Jed is still lending money to my da, which means whenever I make a dent in it, Da's just bringing it back up."

"Your da's a rotten bastard," Chloe hisses. "God, what a prick."

I smile. "Tell me about it. Thankfully, I haven't seen nor heard from him in a while."

Callie's eyes widen. "Ah, that explains why Evie's changed. She's come out of her shell a lot more. She's not afraid to be around people anymore."

"Yeah, they've all come out of themselves. Ma and Da were continuously fighting. It was awful to be around. Now the kids don't need to worry about it. Neither Ma nor Da are allowed back in the house."

Callie pulls me into her arms. "I'm proud of you, Ailbhe. You've taken on a lot. You've helped those kids so much and you're still only young."

I laugh. "I don't feel young. It's hard to believe that I'm eighteen. I feel forty."

"Wait, you're eighteen?" Kane growls from behind me. "The fuck?"

"Uh-oh," Evie says. "You've got to pay up, Preacher, and none of that fake money you have."

I swear to God, this child gets sassier as each day passes. I turn and see Kane reaching into his wallet and pulling out a twenty euro note. "Kid, this is goin' to pay for today, got it?"

Evie looks at the note, almost as though she's contemplating if it's a good deal to make or not. "Okay. But no shouting at Ailbhe."

Kane holds up his hands. "Promise you, kid, I won't

shout at her. But we do need to talk." He reaches for me and pulls me off the chair. I crash against him, but his hands tighten around my hips and he holds me still. "Let's go," he says, his voice rough and low.

"I haven't even eaten," I whine.

"I'll bring it to you," Fiona says as she gets up from her seat, her phone left down on the bar. "Do you want tea too?"

"Yes please. I love you."

She grins at me. "Love you too. Now you two talk and then maybe we can do something today?"

She's been worried about me. They all have. They've not left my side since I came home from the hospital unless they're eating or we're sleeping.

Kane and I go back to my room. "You're eighteen?" he asks.

"I'll be nineteen soon," I assure him. "Why does that matter?"

He stares at me, his gaze searching mine. "I'm twenty-nine, babe."

I lift my shoulders and shrug. "And?" I have no idea what the hell that has to do with anything.

"You don't care?" he questions.

"About what? The ten year age gap?" I ask, and he nods. "No. Look, I'm old enough to make my own decisions, and honest to God, Kane, I knew you were older than me. I didn't know *how* old you were, but honestly, I didn't care. Age is only a number."

The worry leaves his face and his lips curl into a slow smirk. "That's real good, babe, because you're mine, and I ain't letting you go."

"Who said I was yours to hold on to?" I ask, but he's right. I am his. He's all that I want. After our discussion last night, I slept for about an hour, and when I woke up, I cried. I sobbed for the man that has lost so very much. My heart truly hurts for him and how much he's lost. I understand his reasons for wanting a paternity test and for trying to keep his distance. I'm not angry. I'm hurt, but I'm not angry. The way he treated me wasn't right and I think he realizes that.

His chuckle is deep and loud. I love that he's happy. It's almost as though a weight has been lifted from his shoulders. The darkness still lingers in his eyes and I don't think it'll ever fade. He's been through too much for it to disappear. But he's not as wound tight or closed off any longer.

He slams his lips down against mine and he holds me tightly against him. "You're mine, Ailbhe. I've got a lot of shit to make up for, and I swear to fuck, I'll make up for it. I will. But I ain't losin' you." He cradles my face in his hands. "Not knowin' if you were okay or not while I was on that plane was fuckin' torture. All I knew was that Jed had gotten to you. I wasn't sure if you were dead or not. I didn't know if the baby had died—"

I swallow hard, hating that he went through that. "We're fine," I assure him. "We're both doing okay."

"I could have lost you both," he whispers.

I close my eyes, hating that he felt that pain. "We're here," I reply. "Right here with you."

He presses his forehead against mine. "I can't lose you."

I grip a hold of his hands as he continues to cradle my face. "You won't," I promise him.

"I need you to tell me what happened with Jed."

I knew it was coming. I knew he'd want to know about what went down. I quickly tell him everything that happened, trying my hardest not to break down in tears. The last thing I need is for him to realize just how upset I am over the entire ordeal.

Being told by Pyro that I wasn't returning home, and neither were the kids, was a relief. I was scared to go back. I didn't want anything to happen to me or them. I was worried that Jed or his men would return. I'm not sure if I can go back. Not unless the house is secure and it's safe to do so.

"You're tellin' me that this cunt threatened you not once, but on two separate occasions, and you never told anyone?" His words are filled with anger, and I can feel his body vibrating, almost as though he's trying to hold it all inside.

"I didn't have anyone to talk to," I confess quietly. It's a shit thing to admit, but it's true. "Who was I supposed to tell?"

"Me," he growls.

I look up at him and see the anger in those gorgeous brown eyes of his. "It was just sex," I remind him.

He steps back, shoving a hand through his hair, his lip curled into a snarl. "Fuckin' hell, Ailbhe, that cunt threatened to rape you."

"I know," I whisper.

"You could have come to me."

I shake my head, my tears falling. "I couldn't," I whisper. "You played so hot and cold. I couldn't trust you outside of the bedroom, Kane."

A knock at the door has me stepping further back from him.

"Hey, sweetie," I greet as I answer the door. It's Fiona. She's carrying a tray filled with two plates. Right behind her is Chloe, who's got two cups in her hand.

"These are for you and Preacher," Fiona tells me. "We'll let you go back to talking."

I give her a smile as I take the tray from her. I doubt

we'll be talking anymore. I think I've hurt him by my words. I didn't mean to. It was just the truth.

Before I can turn, Kane's there taking the tray from my hands. "I've got it, babe," he says, his words a little rougher than normal.

Damn. I did hurt him. God, I'm such a bitch.

CHAPTER 25
PREACHER

I hadn't realized just how much I had fucked up until I heard her say she didn't trust me. That's the biggest kick in the gut that I've ever had. I would never have sent her away if she'd come to me about Jed and his bullshit. Fuck, that asshole would have died long before he could have hurt her.

"I'm sorry," she tells me, her voice soft and filled with remorse.

She's sitting on the bed, her knees to her chest as she sips on her tea. She's finished her breakfast, and I'm glad to see she's managed to keep it all down. Thankfully, the morning sickness seems to have subsided and she's no longer looking as though she could fall over at the smallest gust of wind.

"What are you apologizing for, babe?" I ask, trying to figure out what the hell she's got to apologize for.

"I didn't mean to hurt you," she says. "I just wanted to be honest."

I shake my head, trying not to smile. Christ, she's so damn fucking sweet. "You didn't hurt me. I'm pissed at myself for bein' such a dick. I shouldn't have kept pushing you away."

"I get why you did. Doesn't mean I liked it. But you had your reasons, Kane. I just hate that you had to go through all that you have."

I don't answer her. There's nothing I can say to that. My past is fucking shit, and it has led me to make some fucked up decisions.

I fucking love that she calls me Kane. I never thought I'd like anyone to use my given name, especially after all the shit that went down with my family. But hearing it from Ailbhe's lips, with that soft Irish lilt... I'll be fucking glad to listen to it for the rest of my life. I know without a fucking shadow of a doubt that I'm going to take her as my old lady. It's going to take a while for us to get to the point where I'll even broach that conversation, but after our discussion last night and then again today, I have a feeling we're on the right path.

First things first, Jed O'Connor is going to die a slow and painful death. Once he's finished with, Peter Mangan is next. There's no fucking way I'll let either of them live to taunt her again. No fucking way. They're done. They've both laid a hurt on her in more ways than one and I'll be damned if they try it again.

"Me and my brothers have a few things to do," I tell her, hoping she won't ask for details. "We'll be gone for a while. This clubhouse is secure and no one is going to hurt you while you're here."

She looks at me with wide eyes. I can see the fear swirling in them.

"You're safe here," I promise her. "I wouldn't leave you and the kids here if I thought you weren't."

She takes a steadying breath and nods. "Okay. Thank you."

"We won't be long," I assure her. "Just got a few things to do, and then once we're finished, we'll be right back." I fucking hate that I'm having to leave her when she's obviously scared, but when I come back, I'll know that she's safe and that no one's going to hurt her again. I came so fucking close to losing her. It won't be happening again.

She rises to her feet and places her cup down on the bedside table. She's a little nervous, but she shuffles closer to me. "Be safe," she whispers as she wraps her arms around my waist.

I reach down and lift her into my arms. Her legs circle my waist, her arms going around my neck. "Look at me," I say thickly.

She raises her head and looks me in the eye. I'm

falling so fucking deep for her. I think I have been since the moment I saw her. She was different to everyone else. She seemed unimpressed, but I knew she wanted me. She didn't make a beeline for me, though. In fact, I went to her. I chased a woman for the first time in my life.

"Never in my life have I had someone care for me the way you have." I press my head against hers. "I'm so fuckin' sorry, baby. The way I treated you wasn't right. It was anythin' but. I'm hopin' there will come a day that you can forgive me."

She shakes her head. "I already have," she says. "I forgave you when you were open and honest with me. I know how much it took for you to do that."

Christ... She gets it. She fucking gets me.

"I won't be long." I slam my lips down against hers. It was supposed to be a quick, hard kiss, but the second she parts her lips, my tongue slides into her mouth. It's hard and fast, and she's grinding against my crotch. If I didn't have somewhere to be, I'd throw her onto the bed and fuck her until she passes out.

Reluctantly, I pull back. She's breathless, her cheeks tinged pink and her chest heaving. "Sorry," she says sheepishly.

"Trust me, babe. I want nothin' more than to fuck you. Get some rest, then if you're up for it tonight, I'll fuck you so hard you'll pass out."

Her cheeks flame even redder. "Kane," she gasps.

I chuckle. She's so fucking sweet and so damn innocent. I nip at her lip, tugging it between my teeth. "Fuck," I hiss. I fucking hate that I have to leave her. This is bullshit, but it's something that needs to be done. I need her safe.

She slides down my body, her body pressing against my thickening cock. "Please be safe, Kane," she whispers.

"You have nothin' to worry about," I tell her.

She gives me a look that tells me she doesn't believe me. "You may think I'm dumb, Kane, but I'm far from it. I know you're going to find Jed. I'm not even going to try and stop you. There's no stopping you, so it would be stupid to try. But he's got a lot of men, and I don't want you to be hurt. So please, I'm begging you, be safe and be careful."

Could she be any fucking sweeter? The woman knows me too damn well and is a fucking lot more understanding than I thought she'd be. I misjudged her, and that's my fault.

"I will. Now get some rest. Whether that's sleepin' or kickin' back and watchin' movies with the kids."

She grins. "Yes, sir," she says sassily.

"You can sir me later on when I'm fuckin' you. Now give me a kiss, babe."

She doesn't hesitate. She reaches up on her tiptoes

and presses a kiss against my lips. Fuck, things are so fucking sweet for me right now. So fucking sweet.

I leave her in our room and make my way downstairs. "About time you showed your face, brother," Reaper says with a grin. "Thought you were goin' to be in bed all day."

I glare at the asshole. "I wish I was," I snarl. "But we've got shit to do and I'm not waitin' around to do it."

Ace nods. "I agree, which is why I made a call and Denis and his boys are waiting for us. They've got a present for you."

I grin. "Then what are we waitin' for?"

We arrive at a secluded farm. I've not been this far out of Dublin before. But it's got a lot of acres and it looks like it would be a great place to build a house and raise a family. Fuck, I'm seeing things so fucking differently now. Especially now that I have my mind solely on Ailbhe and fixing what I have broken.

"Where the fuck are we?" Raptor asks. "Could we be any further from the city?"

Pyro chuckles. "We really could, but, brothers, you're about to witness somethin' fuckin' epic."

We walk round the back of the house, and I'm

shocked to see there's a wood chipper and a fuck ton of plastic on the ground.

"Am I missin' somethin'?" I ask, glancing around, clocking that not only is Denis here, but so are his two sons, Danny and Malcolm, along with Stephen Maguire, Maverick O'Hara, and Freddie Kinnock.

"Preacher," Freddie greets me. "I heard through the grapevine that you're with Ailbhe Mangan?"

"What's it to you?" I ask, wondering what the fuck he's got to do with Ailbhe.

He chuckles. "She's a friend, that's all."

"You always put your foot in it," Maverick grunts. "Preacher, Freddie and Stephen know Ruairi. They have known each other for years. So when Freddie found out that it was Ailbhe who Jed was after, he checked in on her."

"Didn't work out too well now, did it?" Reaper snarls. "Ailbhe was hurt and ended up in hospital. She could have lost the baby."

All the men's faces go slack with shock. They didn't know she was pregnant. I don't think Ailbhe has told anyone other than her siblings.

"So, what's this present you have for me?" I ask, not in the mood to play games any longer.

Stephen smirks. "Alright, Preacher, I get it. You've got a lot to deal with, so Denis here, along with his boys, decided to help you out."

He nods his head, and I watch as Freddie and Maverick move to the side of the house. When they return, I'm shocked to see they each have someone slumped over their shoulders. "Preacher, meet Jed O'Connor and Peter Mangan."

I raise a brow, surprised these men have managed to get the two assholes here. I'm impressed. I smirk when they unceremoniously drop the men to the ground, both of the assholes groaning as they hit the ground with a loud thud.

Damn, that must have hurt.

"Stephen here has a special way of dealing with people. He's willing to let you use that technique. I must warn you, it's fucking brutal," Denis says with a cocky grin.

Now I'm intrigued. "Alright, then," I say, my curiosity getting the better of me. "How about you show me this technique with Peter." Her father practically sold his daughter to Jed. He deserves to die. But I want to be the one who kills Jed.

Stephen wastes no time. He walks over to the wood chipper and switches it on. I watch on with rapt attention as he then proceeds to lift Peter and walk him over to the machine.

"No fuckin' way," Reaper hisses. "No fuckin' way he's goin' to do that."

Oh, but I have a feeling that he is going to drop the

cunt into the machine, and it'll be fun to watch as the bastard is torn to shreds as the machine works him over.

The screams that come from Peter as Stephen pushes him into the wood chipper would have most people running for the fucking hills. It's bone-chilling, haunting, and filled with pain and suffering. The man's howling like it's a full fucking moon.

I watch, completely fascinated, as Peter's arm is torn from his body, blood spurting everywhere, his screams getting louder and even more deranged.

Fuck, this is some sort of torture and I'm all fucking for it. I've never seen something so gory and ugly. It's like something out of a horror movie.

His leg gets sucked in and torn to shreds, just as his arm did before. It's fucking amazing and definitely something we should use in the future.

"It breaks everything up," Denis tells me. "It makes it into next to nothing, and as this is so far away from anything, the wildlife will take whatever's left."

It's fucking ingenious. The man has the perfect killing machine in the best place. It's without a doubt a great torture device. The pain they go through is unlike anything I've ever seen before, nor is it something I can accurately describe.

It takes almost an hour until the majority of Peter's body has gone through the wood chipper. His screams stopped after a few minutes. Between the pain and blood loss, he was dead within minutes.

"My turn," I snap. I've waited long enough to do this and watching as Peter got his comeuppance has only fueled my anger. I reach for Jed and stand him up. He's unsteady on his feet. The fucker's taken a beating. These men didn't go easy on him. Not at fucking all. No wonder the fucker stayed down. He was too injured to get up.

"You," I hiss in his face. "You're going to be in a fuckin' world of pain."

He looks at me with narrowed eyes. "That whore of yours isn't worth it," he snaps.

Oh, this cunt is begging for me to kill him. Wicked fast, I throw a jab to his ribs. He doubles over and coughs as the jab has taken his breath from him. "You don't fuckin' talk about her," I snarl. "You're not worthy to have her name on your lips."

I kick out my leg and smash it down on his shin. The sound of his bone breaking is audible, as is his howl of pain. "I had many ways to kill you, and all would have been messy and painful, but none are as bad as Maguire's device. I'm going to revel in your screams. I'm going to love knowing that you can no longer get to my woman."

"Fuck your whore," he snarls. "She's just another slut. There're many of them."

"You're just jealous that you never had her," I spit. "You never will either."

I'm not listening to any more of his bullshit. No fucking way. He's done. I grab him by the collar and drag the fucker toward the wood chipper. It's still whirring, tearing what little remains of Peter's mangled body. Now it's time for Jed to face his punishment.

With one leg broken, he tries to kick out with the other one. It's no use; he's not strong enough to fight me off. I lift him from the ground and throw him into the machine. It screeches, then I hear the sound of the metal grinding against bones. It's not long before his screams rent the air.

Living out in the countryside has its upsides. No one is around for miles. The downside: who'll be close enough if something happens? For this, it's the perfect place. There's no one to hear him scream. There's no saving him. He signed his death warrant the day he went after my woman.

"You've got to be all sorts of fucked up to have come up with this," Raptor comments.

I chuckle, my eyes never leaving Jed's body, which has been torn to shreds. "Jealous that you didn't come up with the idea yourself, Rap?"

"Don't you fuckin' know it. Who'd have thought we'd find this sort of sick shit here in Ireland? Fuck, I knew I loved this place," he laughs. "But, Maguire, you do this a lot? If so, I want front row seats. This place is a little slow-paced for my likin', but havin' front row seats to this is somethin' I could get behind."

"Not happening," Stephen grunts. "Maybe Maverick will show you his trick one of these days."

"What the fuck do you do, Maverick?" Py asks.

Danny laughs. "All Jerry Houlihan's men have nicknames. Stephen here is the Eraser, Freddie is the Thief, Emmanuel is the Silencer, and Maverick here is called the Cleaner."

My brows knit together. "The Cleaner? What do you do? Clean their bodies or some shit?" Maguire's makes sense. The Eraser—hell, there's nothing left to find of his target's bodies when he's finished with them. Freddie's is obvious. From everything I've heard, he's a very skilled thief and can get into any and all safes.

"Something like that," Maverick says, and I can hear the grin in his voice.

"Once we're finished here, I'll clean this shit up. You go back to Ailbhe," Stephen says to me.

I turn to him, grateful for what he's done. "You ever need anythin', and I mean anythin', I'm here."

He nods. "I'll keep that in mind."

Everyone's silent as Jed's screams start to fade. He's dying and I'm fucking relieved. It's almost over.

His body is being ground into nothing from this

wood chipper. The cops come looking for him, they're never going to find him. Not fucking ever. It's the perfect death.

It takes a further hour and a half until the cunt's body is completely gone. Only tiny bones and flesh are left behind, all things the wildlife will scavenge over the course of the next couple of days. Within a few days, Jed O'Connor will be nothing but a memory.

Reaper slaps my back. "It's done, brother. Ailbhe's safe."

I nod. "She is, and now it's time for me to get back to her." Before I turn to leave, I glance at Freddie. "Any idea where Ruairi is?" I ask. "He hasn't been seen since Ailbhe was released from the hospital and her and the kids came to stay at the clubhouse."

He shakes his head. "Haven't seen him, but I'll track him down."

"You good at trackin' people?" Raptor questions.

Freddie grins. "For a price. What do you need?"

"I'll call you in a few days with the details," Raptor tells him.

He's not giving up hope of finding Mallory. He's determined to find her and I can't blame him. If the tables were turned and it was Ailbhe, I'd use every resource available to me to track her down.

"Sounds good," Freddie says. "First things first, Ruairi."

I nod. "Appreciate it. I'll see you around. Gentlemen, it was good to see you."

We say our goodbyes and I climb onto my bike. It's time to go back to Ailbhe and let her know that she doesn't need to worry any longer.

CHAPTER 26
AILBHE

I'm a nervous wreck as I wait for Kane to return home. I took his advice, and with Mikey's help, we set up a den in the room Hannah and Evie are sharing, and all five of us, Fiona included, have been relaxing as we watch movies. We're on the third installment of Toy Story, and I'm getting worried as time continues to pass without hearing a word from Kane.

"Are we staying here from now on?" Hannah asks me.

I shake my head. As comforting as it is to be here and be surrounded by people who will protect us, I need the kids to be back home and have that stability. So much has changed in such a short amount of time for them, and not to mention I'm pregnant. I can't add more stress by having us live here. I'm going to have to pull on my big girl panties and move back home.

"No, honey, we're going to be going home once the door's fixed properly." It was boarded up when I came home from the hospital. I have a feeling Ruairi did it, but I'm not entirely sure as my brother hasn't been seen since I came home. He left the house while I was in the kitchen and didn't say hello or even check up on me. He's sent me a few text messages letting me know he's okay. I get it. He's feeling guilty. But I don't blame him. Not at all. I just wish he was here so I could tell him that.

"Will Preacher be coming home with us?" she asks, and I feel everyone's gaze turn to me. I focus on the TV, watching Woody and Buzz, hoping my cheeks aren't as red as they feel.

"Why do you ask that?"

"You're having a baby. Don't mams and dads live together?"

"Some do, some don't. It'll be a decision that works for all of us, okay? Right now, I'm not sure what's happening between him and me. I wouldn't move him in the house without talking to all of you first."

"We like him," Fiona says, which shocks me. I turn to her and see that she's smiling softly at me. "He's really trying. We all see that. I don't know what happened between the two of you, but he likes you."

"I like him too, but it's not as easy as that, hon. It's so much harder than us liking one another."

"Do you love him?" Hannah questions.

"Love is something that happens over time," I explain. "I really like him." I'm not sure if I would even know if I had fallen in love. I don't know what it feels like. I've never been in love before. But I do know that even though he's hurt me—not intentionally—he's all that I want. I don't know if that makes me a fool or not, but it is what it is and I'm willing to give us a chance—whatever the hell we are.

"If you wanted him to move in," Mikey says, and I inwardly groan. These kids have definitely been talking. "We wouldn't mind. We just want you to be happy."

I reach for the TV remote and hit pause on the movie. "I am happy. So very much so. You all make me happy and I'm very lucky to have you. What happens between Preacher and I will be taken slowly and you'll know as soon as I do, okay?"

They all nod, and I sigh with relief. Thankfully, that's this conversation over with. I understand that they want me happy and they want me to be with Kane, but I have them to think about and they're my priority. I won't do anything to jeopardize what we've built.

The kids are in bed and Kane returned home hours ago. It's just been hard to get time alone. The moment he walked into the girl's bedroom, I could tell by the look in his eyes that he'd killed Jed. I won't ever ask him about it. While he was gone, I did a lot of thinking, a whole lot of it. If I'm going to be with Kane, there's going to be a lot that I'm not going to know. I've spoken at length with Hayley and Chloe, and they've let me in on the ins and outs of the club. Old ladies don't get to know the ins and outs of club business, and I respect that. So if Kane leaves to do some business, I'll never know what he's done and I'll never ask. I'll continue to pray that he's safe and that he's being careful. That's all I can do.

The bedroom door opens and Kane walks in, his strides long and purposeful. All the while, he keeps his gaze solely on me. "You good?" he asks, his gaze running along my body.

I'm dressed in his tee since I don't have many clean clothes. I didn't pack accordingly. It's the tee he was wearing last night. I snagged it for myself, and the moment I put it on, it felt good against my skin. It's way too big for me but I don't care.

I nod, watching his steps. "He's gone, isn't he?"

His lips twist and he pauses, almost as though he's debating whether or not to tell me. "He's not goin' to bother you again."

I step into his embrace. "Thank you," I breathe, glad that it's over. "What's going to happen to the debt that I owe?"

"You no longer owe your father's debt, babe. That shit's dead in the water."

I rest my cheek against his chest as he holds me tight. "I'm glad you're okay. I was worried about you."

"Shouldn't be, babe. Nothin' was goin' to happen to me. Now, Freddie called. He's been searchin' for Ruairi and found him. He's in a bad way. He's dealin' with a lot of guilt, somethin' I know from experience. Freddie's sortin' his ass out and then he'll be back."

I take a deep breath and release it. Thank God.

"Now," he says thickly. My body reacts to his voice, my blood heating and my stomach clenching. "Where did we leave off before I left?"

My breathing deepens. Damn, I want him. God, I want him so badly that I'm burning for him.

I can feel his erection through his jeans. I'm so turned on right now I can barely think straight. He always manages to get me worked up, always manages to have me feel weak at the knees.

His lips crash against mine, and I can't hold back the moan when his tongue sweeps into my mouth. I'm utterly breathless, clinging to his body. He always makes me feel like a giddy teenager. Our kisses are out of this world. Whenever he gives me all of him, it's as though I'm the only woman in this world. I'm the only one for him.

Tearing his mouth from mine, he takes off his cut and places it on the hook on the bedroom door. I watch as he strips out of his tee and unsnaps his fly. His gaze stays focused solely on me. So much has changed since I was in hospital. It's like he's a changed man. It's as though a switch has been flicked. I'm not complaining. Not in the slightest. This is what I want and I'm praying that this is what he wants too.

He's completely naked, and I decide that now is the right time. I had the prospect do a quick run to my house and collect a few things I needed for the kids. While he was there, he picked up my mail. I grab the letter off the bed and hand it to Kane.

"What is it?" he asks, not once taking his gaze off me.

"The paternity test results."

"What does it say?" he asks, and there's no doubt in his voice. He believes me. This wasn't about that. This was just to stop that past of his from coming back and hurting him again.

"That you're the father," I tell him with a smile as I open the letter and show him.

He tears the letter from my hand and tosses it to the

floor. His hands go to the hem of the tee I'm wearing and he pulls it off my body, dragging it over my head. His lips descend on mine once again and we fall onto the bed. I wrap my legs around his waist. His cock is thick and long as it rubs against my soaked folds. He sinks slowly inside of me, and I bite back a groan. God, it's so fucking good. So slow, but he feels so damn big.

"Kane," I moan, loving having him so deep inside of me.

"Gonna fuck you now, babe."

I nod, my fingers tangling in his hair. I tug hard on it, pulling his lips to mine. He slants his mouth over mine and kisses me. God, this man really knows how to make my body sing. I couldn't imagine being with anyone else. He's what I want. He's all that I want.

He pulls his cock out of me, leaving just the tip. He tears his lips away from mine, and gritting his teeth, he thrusts into me. My body bows at the forceful way he powers into me. I can't stop the cry that spills from my lips as he continues to thrust into me. So forceful, so powerful, so fucking him.

"I'm so full," I cry out. God, the man's going to kill me. But God, what a way it would be to go.

"Fuck," he grunts as he slowly pulls out of me and then thrusts back inside. "How the fuck do you get tighter every damn time?"

"More," I cry out, his cock stretching me as he moves. I love the slight burn that it gives.

"Love fuckin' you, babe. No one compares to you," he rumbles.

My heart soars at his words. Heat pools in my pussy as he pushes my pleasure higher and higher. My orgasm is climbing, and there's no way I'm able to hold it off. "Ahhhh," I cry out as he thrusts deep inside of me.

"That's it, babe. Fuck, yes," he snarls as he thrusts deep once again.

My orgasm tumbles over me and it's his name I scream. He rotates his hips, powering into me over and over again as he chases his own release.

"Kane," I gasp, finding it almost impossible to catch my breath.

"Ailbhe." He groans deeply, pushing into me one last time and coming long and hard.

"It's a good thing I'm already pregnant," I quip. "You seem to lose your mind and completely forget about protection."

"Told you, babe, you drive me crazy, have done since the moment I saw you. I just need to be inside of you. I don't even think. But now that I have you knocked up, I'm going to keep doin' it."

I roll my eyes. God, he's pushing it.

He slowly pulls out of me and collapses onto his

back. He reaches down and pulls the sheets over our naked bodies. "I'm not finished with you yet," he growls as he pulls me into his body. "Gonna give you a little time, babe, but once you're ready, I'm claimin' you."

I laugh. "Think the baby in my belly already shows that you have."

He slaps my arse. "Funny. But I'm claimin' you as my old lady. I want you tied to me forever, babe."

I stare up at him. "I don't know what to say." I'm shocked. "You've changed your tune."

He shakes his head. "Not really. I always knew you were special. I kept pushin' you away 'cause I didn't want to hurt you. I pushed you away to protect us both. It was fucked up, and I'm sorry I hurt you."

I press a kiss to his lips. "No more apologies. I get it. This is our fresh start. Maybe one day you can take me on a date. You know, wine and dine me."

He grins, just as I had wanted him to. "You want romance, babe?"

I lift my shoulder and shrug. "Hey, at least you know I put out."

He pushes me onto my back and presses a kiss to my lips. "Fuckin' phenomenal in bed, babe. I swear, you're the most beautiful woman I've ever set eyes on."

My breath catches at his words. "Well, handsome, you're not so bad yourself."

"Thanks for givin' me another chance."

God, he's killing me. "Don't make me regret it."

He looks so fierce. "Never," he vows.

I pray that he's right, but I have a feeling that things are going to be plain sailing for us from here on out.

I've found my prince charming, and he rides a Harley.

CHAPTER 27
PREACHER

TEN WEEKS LATER

"Here you go, brother," Pyro says with a broad grin as he hands me the property of patch.

Today's the fucking day. I get to claim my woman and we get to find out what gender our baby is.

I grin. "Thanks, Prez," I say, proud that I finally have this. As promised, I waited until Ailbhe was ready. She's more than that now.

The past ten weeks have been different than anything I could have anticipated. Things between Ailbhe and I are better than ever. I'm so fucking in love with her that I can't think straight. She's become so important to me that I finally understand what my brothers mean when they talk about their old ladies. I finally have that. I never would have dreamed that this would be true, but coming to Ireland was the best thing for me.

The saying that everything happens for a reason is true. Having Tyson for the little time that I did was to put me in the right frame of mind to be a father. To finally grow up and become the man I was supposed to be. It's paved the way for me to be who I am now.

My life has changed so much in the past ten weeks. I'm with the woman I love and helping her raise her siblings. Yes, all four of them. The kids got used to our relationship quicker than Ailbhe and I did. For the both of us, this is our first and only relationship, and we're learning as we go. But the kids are important to Ailbhe, and so in turn have become important to me. They may be crazy but they're family now. I haven't moved in with them, but I do spend every night with them. Whether that be at their house or them staying at the clubhouse. I know what I want and that's my family. I won't spend a night without them.

I say goodbye to Pyro and move toward my truck. Ailbhe's halfway through her pregnancy now and we're finally going to find out the gender. Whenever we've gone before, the baby's not been co-operating at all. Today, though, we're not leaving until we find out.

I place the patch in my pocket as I climb into the truck. I've got just over an hour to meet her at the hospital for the scan. Ruairi and Mikey want a boy, whereas the girls want another girl in the house. I just want Ailbhe and the baby to be healthy. Either gender would be perfect. I know Ailbhe feels the exact same as me. She just wants everything to run smoothly.

My fingers tap the steering wheel in rhythm to the music playing in the truck. I'm an inpatient fuck, always have been. Now that I have the property of patch, I want to give it to Ailbhe right away. I want her to wear it. She's unable to get a tattoo until after the baby is born. We've had multiple discussions about her becoming my old lady and she's determined to get a tattoo. She's seen pictures of all the other old ladies tattoos and wants to have her own. She's even asked Fiona to design it when the time comes.

Her sister is an amazing artist, and Ailbhe is encouraging her to pursue that dream. Ruairi finally pulled his ass out of his head. It took him almost a week, but he finally came to see her. He apologized, and Ailbhe threatened to kick him in the balls if he said sorry once more. She told him it wasn't his fault. Something I highly disagree with. She gave him the money to pay the debt. What he did with that money, I doubt we'll ever know. She worked her ass off for that, and he fucked up and Ailbhe paid the price. He's taken accountability for his actions and has assured her he'll never do anything like that again.

He won't get the fucking chance. I'll kill him before he could try.

The kids haven't asked about their father. No one has seen him in a while. Even before we killed him, he hadn't been seen in months. From what I've overheard Ailbhe and Ruairi say, they believe he's gone to England. I'm going to let them believe that. I don't want Ailbhe to feel the guilt of knowing her father's dead. She'll only blame herself, when the man only had himself to blame.

The Gallaghers have earned massively from Jed's death. They've taken over his business, giving us part ownership of the apartment blocks he once owned. Denis' daughter-in-law Melissa did a thorough background check on the buildings. A developer got into a lot of debt with Jed, and in turn, lost every apartment complex he owned to the asshole.

We've spent the past month having each apartment renovated to a high standard and ensuring there's adequate security on each building. We've been able to up the rent and it's bringing in a decent monthly sum. There were fourteen apartment buildings in total. Denis had wanted to split it between the Fury Vipers, the Gallaghers, and then with Freddie, Maverick, and Stephen. But shit went south between Stephen and

Denis' wives for a while, and they ended up in danger. It was a huge clusterfuck. In the end, Denis and Stephen called in every favor they could. They had the entire backing of the Houlihan gang, the Gallaghers, the Fury Vipers, the Gallos, and the Devil Falcons MC. It was brutal. Stephen's currently hauled up in the country with his wife while they recover, while Denis is staying close to Callie as is her brother.

I reach the hospital, and I can't stop the grin when I see Ailbhe waiting for me at the door. She's even sexier than ever. The bump she has is small and her boobs have grown. She complains that they're heavy, and I hate that she's struggling, but I can't deny how fucking great they look.

"Babe," I call out once I'm close.

She turns, and that blinding smile of hers is so fucking perfect, it lights up her entire face. "Hey, handsome, everything go okay?"

I reach into my pocket as I nod. "Yep. I wanted to give you this." I hand her the patch and watch as her eyes widen and fill with tears. I guessed she'd be overwhelmed with emotion.

"Kane," she whispers. "Are you sure?"

I roll my eyes. This woman has no fucking idea just how much she means to me. I pull her into my arms. "Listen to me, babe. You're the only woman I want. You're my old lady now and there's no changin' it. I fuckin' love you, and I'm proud that you're my old lady."

Her lips part and her tears continue to fall. "You love me?" she questions. "Really?"

I frame her face with my hands. "I fuckin' love you."

She blinks furiously, almost as though she's trying to stop the tears from falling. "I love you too."

My heart swells, and that heaviness that's been settled on my chest eases. Christ... She has no fucking idea what it means to hear those words leave her lips. I slam my mouth against hers, cursing the fact we're in public. Had we been at home, I'd be balls deep inside of her.

"Let's go see our baby, then we can go home and celebrate," she tells me as she wipes away her tears.

"Sounds like a fuckin' plan."

She sighs. "You're going to have to stop cursing, Kane. You've practically paid for a year's college for Evie already."

I chuckle. She's not fucking wrong. "Who taught her to ask for money?" Whoever the hell it was is a damn asshole. That child is an evil genius and she's only six. She's going to rule the world when she's older, that's for damned sure.

"Mikey," Ailbhe replies, sounding exhausted. "He teaches them everything. But please try to ease up on the cursing."

I shake my head. "Not goin' to happen."

She throws her hands up. "Whatever. Don't complain to me when she bankrupts you."

I slide my arm around her shoulders, pulling her into me. "Come on, babe, let's go see our baby."

It takes a while for us to get called back. It's her twenty-week scan so the nurse is measuring the baby and ensuring everything's okay. My eyes are glued to the screen. I'm utterly fascinated watching my baby move around as the nurse moves the wand over Ailbhe's stomach.

"Are you ready to find out the gender?" the nurse asks after what feels like hours.

I glance at Ailbhe, wanting to make sure she's all for this, but my woman's already nodding her head, smiling brightly.

"You're having a boy. Everything is measuring correctly. He's growing perfectly."

A weight has been lifted off my shoulders. Knowing how Tyson was when he was born, this is going to be completely different. Ailbhe and Pepper are night and day. There's no doubt in my mind that Ailbhe would never do anything to put our child in harm's way.

I press a kiss to my woman's lips. "Thank you, baby," I say, still in awe of the fact I have a baby on the way. I ran from New York after losing a child, and now just over a year later, I'll be having another. It's fucking crazy.

"I can't wait for everyone to find out. They're all going to be so happy."

She's not wrong. My brothers have been taking bets on what we're having. I can't complain; I've done it plenty of times in the past when my brothers were having their own kids. I know Reaper has money on our baby being a boy. Looks as though he's cashing in.

"So?" Py asks as Ailbhe and I take a seat. We're back at the clubhouse, and everyone's here, including all of Ailbhe's siblings, not to mention the Gallaghers, Freddie and Maverick. "Don't leave us in suspense any longer."

Chuckling comes from the laptop that's set up on the bar. The brothers in New York are also with us. They're waiting for the news just as those who are here are.

I've been sober for almost three months now, and I haven't once thought about having a drink. It's crazy to me how much I have missed by constantly being a drunken mess. I have a lot of people who give a shit about me and I took it for granted when I was in New

York. Not any longer. I'm fucking grateful to have so many people in my life.

"It's a boy," I tell them, my chest filled with pride. I'm so fucking happy.

Cheers sound throughout the clubhouse and over the laptop. Everyone's celebrating and joyful. I pull Ailbhe onto my lap and press a kiss to her lips. "Love you, babe."

She grins at me. "I love you too, Kane, and I really want to call the baby Emmet Abel Mangan. I want to give you a name that's not tainted by your parents."

"Fuck," I whisper. Christ, this woman never fails to shock me. Not fucking ever. "You good with that?"

She nods. "So good with it."

"You marryin' me then, Ailbhe?"

"I am your old lady, right?"

Damn fucking straight she is.

Before I can say anything, the doors to the clubhouse crash open and a woman stumbles in. Her face is a mess, she's covered in blood, and she's holding her arm close to her chest.

"Raptor," she croaks. "Help." She crumples to the floor.

"Mallory?" Raptor growls as he moves toward her, his face twisted with rage as he watches the woman he's been looking for passed out on the ground.

Fuck. What the fuck happened?

GLOSSARY

Here's a glossary of how to pronounce some of the names in this book:

Ailbhe: pronounced: Al-vuh
Ruairi: pronounced: Rory
Fiadh: pronounced: Fee-A
Bronagh: pronounced: Bro-na
Aoibheann: pronounced: Av-een
Bláithín: pronounced: Bla-hin
Sadhbh: pronounced: Si-ve

ARE YOU READY FOR MORE?

Raptor and Mallory's book is up next!

Raptor met the woman of his dreams in Pyro's book, he's been looking for her ever since. Now she's back and it's up to Raptor to save her.

BOOKS BY BROOKE:

The Kingpin Series:

Forbidden Lust

Dangerous Secrets

Forever Love

The Made Series:

Bloody Union

Unexpected Union

Fragile Union

Shattered Union

Hateful Union

Vengeful Union

Explosive Union

Cherished Union

Obsessive Union

Gallo Famiglia:

Ruthless Arrangement

Ruthless Betrayal

Ruthless Passion

The Houlihan Men of Dublin:

The Eraser

The Cleaner

The Fury Vipers MC NY Chapter:

Stag

Mayhem

Digger

Ace

Pyro

Shadow

Wrath

Reaper

The Fury Vipers MC Dublin Chapter:

Preacher

Raptor

Standalones:

Saving Reli

Taken By Nikolai

A Love So Wrong

OTHER PEN NAMES

Stella Bella

(A forbidden Steamy Pen name)

Taboo Temptations:

Wicked With the Professor

Snowed in with Daddy

Wooed by Daddy

Loving Daddy's Best Friend

Brother's Glory

Daddy's Curvy Girl

Daddy's Intern

His Curvy Brat

His Curvy Temptress

Daddy's Devilish Girl

Twisted Daddy

Seduced by Daddy's Best Friend

Stepbrother Seduction

Taboo Teachings:

Royally Taught

Extra Curricular with Mr. Abbot

Forbidden Bosses:

Conveniently Yours

Bred by Daddy

Gilded Billionaire

Maid for Love

ABOUT BROOKE SUMMERS:

USA Today Bestselling Author Brooke Summers is a Mafia Romance author and is best known for her Made Series.

Brooke Summers was born and raised in South London. She lives with her daughter and hubby.

Brooke has been an avid read for many years. She's a huge fan of Colleen Hoover and Kristen Ashley.

Brooke has been dreaming of writing for such a long time. When she was little, she would make up stories just for fun. Seems as though she was destined to become an author.

WANT TO KNOW MORE ABOUT BROOKE SUMMERS?

Check out her website:
www.brookesummersbooks.com

Subscribe to her newsletter: www.brookesummersbooks.com/newsletter